BUCKLE
and
SQUASH

and the
Land of the Giants

✔ KU-488-709

34 4124 0007 9259

Books by Sarah Courtauld

Buckle and Squash and the Monstrous Moat-Dragon

Buckle and Squash and the Land of the Giants

BUCKLE and SQUASH

and the Land of the Giants

SARAH COURTAULD

MACMILLAN CHILDREN'S BOOKS

First published 2015 by Macmillan Children's Books
an imprint of Pan Macmillan
20 New Wharf Road, London N1 9RR
Associated companies throughout the world
www.panmacmillan.com

ISBN 978-1-4472-5557-4

Text and illustrations copyright © Sarah Courtauld 2015

The right of Sarah Courtauld to be identified as the
author and illustrator of this work has been asserted by her in
accordance with the Copyright, Designs and Patents Act 1988.

All rights reserved. No part of this publication may be reproduced,
stored in a retrieval system, or transmitted, in any form or by any means
(electronic, mechanical, photocopying, recording or otherwise),
without the prior written permission of the publisher.

1 3 5 7 9 8 6 4 2

A CIP catalogue record for this book is available from
the British Library.

Printed and bound by CPI Group (UK) Ltd, Croydon CR0 4YY

This book is sold subject to the condition that it shall not,
by way of trade or otherwise, be lent, resold, hired out,
or otherwise circulated without the publisher's prior consent
in any form of binding or cover other than that in which
it is published and without a similar condition including this
condition being imposed on the subsequent purchaser.

For Layla

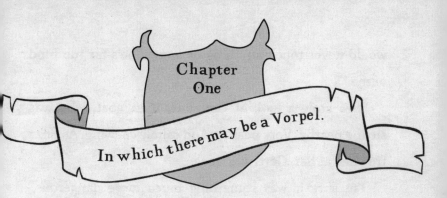

'Gurgling Goblins. Venomous Vorpels. Monstrous Murgs,' Grandma Maud told Eliza. 'It could have been any of them.'

They were standing in the garden behind Old Tumbledown Farm. Grandma Maud was scowling as she pointed her stick at a jumper on the washing line. Well, it used to be a jumper. Now it was more of an oversized flannel. Both its arms and most of its body appeared to have been eaten overnight.

'It could have been Gertrude,' said Eliza.

'Gertrude?'

'That ate your jumper.'

'Nonsense, child!' said Grandma Maud. 'That goat

1

would never touch anything of mine. She's far too fond of me.'

Eliza stole a look at Gertrude, their goat, who was sitting nearby. Very nearby. And calmly chewing. As Eliza frowned at her, Gertrude froze.

'I'm sure it was something much more dangerous,' Grandma Maud went on. 'When it returns, I dare say that will be the end of us.'

'Well, not if I have anything to do with it,' said Eliza.

She'd been practising with her new bow and arrow for days. Now she held up her bow, placed the arrow, pulled back the string, shut one eye, aimed at her target – a piece of parchment tacked to a nearby tree – and let the arrow fly.

PEOW!

The arrow soared through the air, towards the tree, past the tree, on a bit, then climbed high into the air, before finally plunging down into the woods beyond the end of the garden. There was an unfortunate squawk.

'I wouldn't bother with your bow and arrow, dear,' said Grandma Maud. 'If a Vorpel decides to eat us, it will simply eat us.'

Hmmmn. If something *did* come to attack the farm, Eliza didn't want to end up as its dinner, or even its pre-dinner snack. There were plenty of man-eating creatures in the forests of Squerb: Diabolical Dragons, Grofulous Ghouls, the Dread Vole of Gweem, the Very Surprising Caterpillar, the Even More Surprising Slice of Ham – and Eliza wasn't going to let them get her, or her family. So she spent the rest of the morning practising with her bow and arrows. Soon the garden was dotted with arrows. There were arrows in barrows. Arrows in marrows. Arrows in the nests of worried-looking sparrows. In fact, there was only one place where there *weren't* any arrows – and that was in the target.

Dread Vole of Gweem.

Meanwhile, Grandma Maud was reading aloud from one of her favourite books: *Five Hundred Signs that the World is About to End.* Occasionally she beckoned Eliza over, to read out a particularly frightening entry.

'Venomous Vorpels,' she said excitedly, 'are highly dangerous creatures, that will appear before The End of Time. They can be identified by their long grey tendrils— Quick!' she shrieked. 'There! A Vorpel! Fire!'

Eliza looked up. Beyond the hedge at the end of the garden, there *was* a long grey tendril floating in the air. She aimed, fired and, for the first time that day, hit her target.

Unfortunately, or perhaps fortunately, her target turned out not to be a Venomous Vorpel. Or even a Vaguely Villainous Vorpel. It was just Nora, an old lady who lived in the local village, The Middle of Nowhere.

'Morning!' Nora waved cheerfully. She appeared not to have noticed the arrow that was now nestling in her hair. 'Are you coming to hear the news?'

'Grandma, should I say something?' asked Eliza, under her breath.

A Vorpel

Not a Vorpel

'Not at all, that would be most impolite,' Grandma Maud murmured. 'What news?' she asked more loudly.

'There's a royal announcement happening in the village,' said Nora.

'I'll see you there, Nora,' said Eliza.

'Royal news,' said Grandma Maud, shaking her head. 'It's probably nothing important.' Then her eyes lit up. 'Unless it's The End of the World! Could well be. After all, it *is* written that the world will end on a cloudy day.'

'Um, where is that written, Grandma?'

'It is written in a notebook,' said Grandma Maud, 'a notebook that I just wrote it in.'

Personally, Eliza didn't really care about the royal family. It was

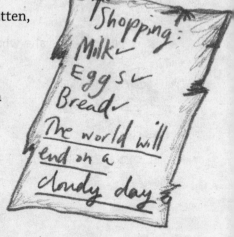

Eliza's sister, Lavender, who loved that sort of thing. For a moment, Eliza wondered where her sister was. For Lavender was very, very far away . . .

At last, Lavender thought. At last she was where she belonged. Once, she had just been a poor, humble and incredibly talented young girl who lived with her family on a small farm in The Back of Beyond. But now, finally, Lavender was exactly where she deserved to be. She was standing in a ballroom, gazing into the eyes of her one true love.

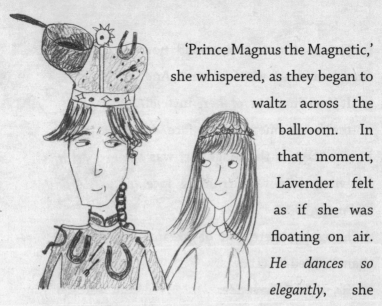

'Prince Magnus the Magnetic,' she whispered, as they began to waltz across the ballroom. In that moment, Lavender felt as if she was floating on air. *He dances so elegantly*, she thought, *in spite of all the nails, horseshoes and iron chains stuck to his chest and arms*. As the dance drew to a close, Prince Magnus the Magnetic smiled, leaned towards her, and whispered:

'LAVENDER?! LAVENDER! LAVENDER!!!'

Lavender looked up.

Suddenly the ballroom vanished, and Lavender found herself back in the yard behind her home. Instead of the fragrance of roses, she could now smell a distinct whiff of mud. And goat. And in front of her, instead of the handsome, smiling face of Prince Magnus the Magnetic, was the frowning, intensely irritating face of her sister, Eliza.

'Lavender, were you daydreaming again?' asked Eliza.

'Er, no,' said Lavender.

'Have you washed Gertrude yet?'

'Er, yes,' said Lavender.

'Really?' said Eliza. 'Because she looked muddy this morning, and she looks even muddier now. Also, were you waltzing with her?'

'Er, no.'

'And why is she wearing a crown?'

'Is she?' said Lavender. 'I didn't notice. How strange.'

Eliza sighed. 'Well, do you want to come and hear the Village Crier? Apparently, he has some royal news.'

'ROYAL NEWS!' said Lavender. 'Why didn't you tell me?'

'I just did,' said Eliza.

'Well then, why are you holding us up?'

'I'm not,' said Eliza.

'You are! You are holding us up, with all this conversation! We should be running, not talking!'

'But you're the one who's talking.'

'But you're the one who started it!'

'But does that even matter?'

'NO!'

Then Lavender was off, skipping all the way to the village. While she skipped, she sang. Like many of her songs, this one had many words, and no tune whatsoever.

> *'A palace is my destiny,*
> *That's where my prince will wait for me*
> *He'll bring me joy and scones for tea,*

Our happiness will spread you see,

Just like jam – or leprosy

(But it won't be quite so itchy)

And we will sing in harmony

In a perfect key

(That's not rusty)

The key of eeeeeeeeeeeeeeee

eeeeeeeeeeeeeeeeeeee

eeeeeeeeeeeeeeeeeeeeeee

eeeeeeeeeeeeeeeeeeeeeeeeee!

Because a palace is my destiny.'

As Lavender skipped and sang, and villagers flew from her, shaking their heads and clutching their ears, Eliza ran along beside her, smiling contentedly. She loved it when her sister sang, because it made her feel proud. Proud of her latest invention: gobbets of candlewax that she put in her ears so she couldn't hear a single note of Lavender's hideous singing.

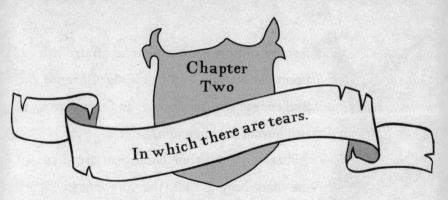

Chapter Two

In which there are tears.

By the time Eliza and Lavender reached the village square, Steve, the Village Crier, was already crying.

'Oooooohhh! Urghhhhhh! Warghhhhhh!!!!' he bawled. 'Urghhh! Ooooww!! Auuurghhh!!!!!' He wept, bawled, wailed and blubbed, until everyone had arrived. When the whole village was gathered, he blew his nose, looked up, and beamed.

'Good morrow, fine citizens of Squerb!' he said. 'Today I bring wondrous news from our fair capital, Letters. This morning, a royal wedding has taken place!'

Lavender's eyes widened. She gripped her sister's hand. She adored royal weddings. One day, *she* was going to marry a prince, and have a royal wedding of her own. It was

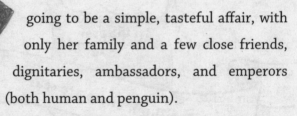

going to be a simple, tasteful affair, with only her family and a few close friends, dignitaries, ambassadors, and emperors (both human and penguin).

Eliza, on the other hand, just frowned. She had hoped that the announcement would at least be about something vaguely interesting – like the day Prince Nigel the Intrepid had announced that he was off to hunt the Dread Vole of Gweem. Or the day after that, when Prince Nigel had announced that the Dread Vole of Gweem was just fine, and anyway, it only ate people on Tuesdays, so really, it was perfectly all right to leave it just where it was. And no, he wasn't scared of it. Of course not. Why would anyone think that?

'My friends,' Steve declared, 'this very morning, the world's third biggest, and only Mass Surprise Royal Wedding has taken place! On this happy morn, all fifty Princes of Squerb and the surrounding kingdoms were married, to forty-nine princesses, and one very lucky sheep.

'After the ceremony, Princess Kristina, one of the brides, walked among the crowds, sharing her special story. "It was wonderful," she said. "I love my new husband, and there is no way that I married him just because he was a prince. I definitely remember his name. I could easily find him again, amongst all these other princes. Actually, has anyone seen him? He's called . . . um . . . er. He looks . . . kind of . . . royal-ish?"

'And so, dear friends, there will be no more royal weddings in Squerb for many, many years to come, for now all the princes and princesses in the realm are happily married.'

As the villagers burst into cheers, and Steve, the Village Crier, burst into tears (again), Eliza turned to her sister, and noticed that she had turned pale. She was even paler than this page.

Unlike this page, Lavender didn't have words written on her. But if she *had* had words written on her, they would have been words like:

WHAT?

and

NO!

and

ARGHHHHHHHHHH!!

'Lavender,' said Eliza. 'Are you all right? Maybe you should sit down.'

'Shhh!' Lavender replied. 'I'm listening!'

Because now the Village Crier was reading out all the names of the princes who had got married. '. . . Prince Harry the Invincible, Prince Larry the Vincible, Prince Aethelred the Unready and his brothers Prince Aethelred the Nearly Ready and Prince Aethelred The Hang On, I'll Be There In Just A Sec, Prince Nigel the Intrepid, Prince Magnus the Magnetic—'

'No!' Lavender cried.

'. . . Prince Roland the Incontinent, Prince Antarctic the Continent, Prince Vlad the Impaler, Prince Brad the Impala, Prince Alice the Pretender . . .'

14

When he got to the end of the list, Lavender beamed. 'There's still a prince that I can marry! He still hasn't mentioned Prince Ian the Princely! I will set my heart on him.'

'And in other news,' said the Village Crier, 'Prince Ian the Princely has given up his title, and run away to paint ducks. After a short and moving ceremony the artist formerly known as Prince Ian the Princely said: "I hated being a prince. I'm off and you'll never find me! Bye!"'

Then Steve gave the traditional signal that the royal announcement was over. 'The royal announcement is over,' he announced.

As the other villagers started to wander away, Lavender stood there, completely still, as if time had stopped. Actually, as if time had stopped, sat down, had a cup of tea, and another one, and then gone for a bit of a snooze.

Time

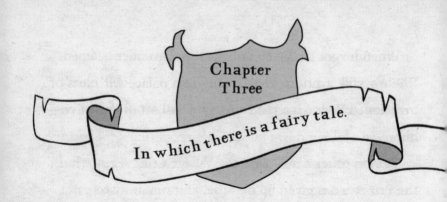

'Um . . . Lavender?' said Eliza. 'Come on, let's go home.'

But Lavender didn't move an inch.

'Who needs princes anyway?' said Eliza. 'Princes are boring! They spend all their lives opening monasteries, and visiting leper colonies. And they never have any fun, because there are always scribes following them around, just waiting to make illuminated manuscripts of them if they catch them doing anything embarrassing.'

But Lavender did not respond.

'You weren't really ever going to marry a prince, were you? Realistically,' said Eliza. 'Statistically, you're more likely to be run over by a cow. Or catch the Black Death.'

If this was supposed to cheer Lavender up, it didn't

work. She continued to stare into space.

'Anyway, who says that living in a palace with lots of rooms, and dresses, and servants is better than living here, in a falling-down house with a roof that's collapsing, and Vorpels that might come out of the forest and attack us at any moment?'

Still nothing from Lavender.

Eliza frowned. 'That didn't come out quite how I meant it to,' she said. 'But the point is – this is your home. And we're your family. You belong here. You don't need to be rescued by a stupid prince. So really, everything's fine.'

Lavender started walking slowly off along the path, in the direction of their home. But she still didn't say a word.

That afternoon, while Eliza practised vanquishing imaginary Vorpels with her catapult, Lavender was still completely silent. She didn't even cheer up for Grandma Maud's 'End of the World' tea party.

'It's coming!' said Grandma Maud, with an enormous

smile on her face. 'The end is nigh! Go on. Have a teacake while you can.'

But Lavender didn't have a teacake. She just sat there looking glum, and only nodded blankly when Grandma Maud announced that she was off to find a lovely spot to watch The End of the World. And she'd be back in a couple of days. Or not at all, depending on how The End of the World went.

After supper, Lavender still hadn't spoken. So, as she sat by herself in the yard, Bonnet decided to go and try to cheer her up, by telling her a story.

But wait! Bonnet? Who is this person, 'Bonnet'? Is he a

man? Is he a type of hat? Is he a hero?

If you haven't met Bonnet before, here are a few things you should know about him. To start with, he's scared of many things. 3,173 at the last count, including werewolves, spiders, caves, tortoises, heights, Thursdays, pigeons, sandwiches without cucumber in them and the colour mauve.

Secondly, though he was small and shaped roughly like a scone, Bonnet was actually a giant. He was just not the same size as his brothers and sisters.

He was not fond of hitting things, or smashing things, or biting things, like his brothers and sisters were. But he definitely *was* a giant. His giant family had always told him so. 'Ha ha ha ha – you're such a rubbish giant!' they used to say, while affectionately hitting him over the head with a very large club.

Thirdly, having left the Land of the Giants, Bonnet now lived with Lavender, Eliza, Grandma Maud and Gertrude, in The Back of Beyond. They had taken him in when he was lost and lonely, and they were all very fond of him. Lavender and Eliza made him feel at home, by being his friends. Gertrude made him feel at home, by eating his socks. And Grandma Maud made him feel at home, by saying things like: 'Pass the milk, would you, Bucket?'

So, that's Bonnet.

'Hello, Lavender,' Bonnet said, sitting down beside her.

'Hmmn,' she said.

Hmmn wasn't much. But it was something, Bonnet thought. So he kept going.

'Maybe I could, um, cheer you up, with a fairy tale?'

said Bonnet. He knew that Lavender loved fairy tales.

'Hmmmnn,' said Lavender, with a shrug.

'Once upon a time,' Bonnet said. 'Once upon a time, there was a . . . door. It was a happy door. And it was . . . green. The End.'

He decided to start again.

'Once upon a time, there was a beautiful bird. It was magical – so magical that it could fly! Er, just like . . . er, most other birds.'

This really wasn't going well. Bonnet looked down at his hands. He twiddled his thumbs. He decided to try one last time . . .

'Once upon a time, there was a tiny girl,' he said, 'a girl as small as a thumb. She had magical powers, and she lived in a muddy yard . . .'

'No she didn't!' Lavender suddenly replied. 'If she was magical, she DEFINITELY did not live in a muddy yard. Let *me* tell it. Once upon a time, there was a girl who was tiny and magical. She lived in a fairy kingdom, just like in *Thumbelina*, and she met a tiny prince, who was just the same size as her, and they fell in love and – that's it!'

Lavender leaped to her feet.

'That's what?' said Bonnet.

'That's the answer! Thanks, Bonnet!' said Lavender, planting a kiss on his head, and a daisy in the grass – that's how excited she was.

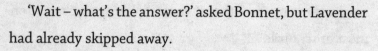

'Wait – what's the answer?' asked Bonnet, but Lavender had already skipped away.

Bonnet sighed. He didn't know what the answer was. He didn't even know what the question was. All he knew was that when he spent time with Lavender, he often found himself feeling a bit light-headed.

He decided to add another worry to his list of worries.

Worry no. 3,174: Could I be allergic to Lavender?

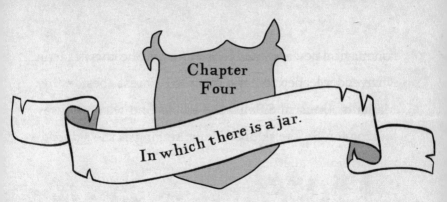

Chapter Four

In which there is a jar.

As she skipped along past The Back of Beyond, through The Side of Beyond, and then into the Haunted Forest, Lavender was grinning from ear to ear. Of course! She had thought that the world had completely run out of princes. She had thought that her life was over, and she was going to be stuck living on a boring farm forever. But she couldn't have been more wrong! Lavender wasn't going to marry a normal, boring, *human* prince. Who wanted one of those, anyway?

Real princes were all right, she thought. *But MAGICAL PRINCES – they were much better.* Lavender was going to fall in love with a magical prince, who lived in a magical kingdom. All she needed to do was to find someone who had magical powers – and that was easy. She knew exactly where to go. Beyond the Haunted Forest, beside The Marsh of Unusual Smells, she would find what she was looking for. So she skipped along, singing as she skipped.

And as she sang, all the ghostly nettles, phantom acorns and eerie daffodils in the Haunted Forest fled from the sound of her voice.

'I'm going to be tiny
So small and so sweet,
So tiny, so small, so sweet and petite
Smaller than a pigeon, puffin or a parakeet
Smaller than a mushroom or a single grain of wheat
Smaller than a slice of ham or any other meat
And in a fairy kingdom then my fairy prince I'll meet
And in a tiny palace on a tiny fairy street –
We'll foxtrot round our ballroom on our very tiny feet
And tiny five-course banquets, with tiny forks we'll eat –
For I'm going to be tiny, a tiny prince to meeeeeeeet.'

25

Soon enough, she had run through the forest, and come to the edge of The Marsh of Unusual Smells. Right beside the marsh, there was a small cottage, with a purple plume of smoke rising from the chimney, and a sign on the door that read:

BORIS THE WITCH
Enter ~~if you dare!~~
through the door.

BUT WAIT!

Stop!

Arrêt (as they say in France).

Lopettaa (as they say in Finland).

Nimini nimini footledroop (as they say in my kitchen, just a second ago).

You may be thinking: doesn't this book have GIANTS in the title?

Were they all so TALL that they just didn't fit in the book? Did they all get such sore necks from trying to fit into such a small book that they left and went to live in the *Very Tall Book of Very Tall Buildings* instead?

Did the illustrator of this book just decide to replace all the giants in this book with question marks, because they are much, much easier to draw?

Well, no. The giants will turn up soon enough. And when they do, you'll probably wish they hadn't.

Anyway, the door to the cottage was a jar.

Odd.

Lavender stepped over it, and went inside. Standing in the gloomy room before her were three women. One was old and wrinkled and skinny as a twig. One had fiery red hair, that came bursting out of her head like a child's scribble. And one was just a little girl. They were all wearing spiky witches' hats, long witches' robes and bright witches' grins.

'Does Boris the witch live here?' asked Lavender.

'I am she!' replied the woman with the fiery hair. 'These are my weird sisters, Doris and Horace.'

(Horace was the wrinkly, old one. Doris was the little girl.)

'We're not *really* weird,' said Doris.

'And we're not really sisters,' added Horace.

'Hello, Boris, Doris and Horace,' said Lavender. 'Boris, I think you borrowed my sister's knees once.'

'Ah, yes! And lovely knees they were too. How can I be of service to you?'

Lavender paused for a moment, taking in the strange scene before her. The walls were covered with shelves and shelves of strange, slimy things in jars, and shelves and shelves of strange, slimy things that definitely *should* have been in jars.

29

In one corner, there was a pile of broomsticks, which Lavender sort of expected, and in another corner there was a pile of rabbits, which she definitely didn't.

'I have come from afar, seeking a magical spell,' said Lavender, trying her best to sound mysterious and important, and like the kind of person a witch would like to help.

'Of course,' said Boris. 'For I knew, before you even stepped into this room, what it was that brought you here.'

'You did?'

'I did.'

'Really?'

'Definitely.'

'But that's so magical!'

All seeing pie

'But of course,' said Boris. 'For I have the gift of foresight. I looked deep into the future, with the help of my all-seeing pie, and I saw all. But tell me anyway, in your own words.'

'Well, I want to become tiny,' said Lavender.

'What?! Why?!' spluttered Boris. 'I mean, of course you do. Go on.'

'I want to become tiny, so I can go to a faraway kingdom, and fall in love with a tiny, magical prince.'

'Oh, don't we all, don't we all,' said Boris. 'But what can you give me, in return for such a priceless gift? A vial of magical elixir? A crystal ball? An invisible unicorn?'

Lavender thought for a moment. 'What about an *imaginary* unicorn?' she said, imagining one on the spot.

'Perhaps,' said Boris. 'What colour is it?'

'Purple,' said Lavender.

'Purple?!' Boris sounded disappointed. 'You didn't imagine a green one?'

'Er, no.'

'That is a great shame,' said Boris. 'Well, there's nothing we can do about that now. What else can you give me?'

'I've got . . . a silver coin, a red button and, er, I'm not sure what this is,' she said, delving into her pockets. 'I think it might have once been fudge?'

'That's it?' said Boris.

'Oh, and I could sing you a song if you like? I can make one up right now!'

She cleared her throat.

> '*Sisters three, they're all quite weird,*
> *With hats and warts and is that a beard?*'

'Enough!' thundered Boris. But Lavender was just getting into her stride.

> '*And while they cast each magic spell*
> *Many rabbits here do dwell*
> *Are they magical as well?*
> *Or do they just look sweet, and smell . . .*'

32

'ENOUGH!' said Boris, who was now shaking all over, and had her fingers in her ears.

'But I had eight more verses!' said Lavender.

'Your singing is powerful indeed,' said Boris. 'I'm sure we can come to some kind of arrangement. Doris!' she cried. 'This child has an urgent request. Fetch the Holy Snail!'

At this, Doris nodded, hopped over a few stray rabbits, scurried to the back of the room, opened a trapdoor, and disappeared into the cellar below. A few moments later, she returned with a small wooden box in her hands, and handed it to Boris.

'In this box is the Holy Snail,' Boris said solemnly. 'It contains a deep and powerful magic. Behold!'

Boris opened the box, and Lavender peered inside. Sitting in the box, quietly nibbling on a piece of lettuce, was a small, brown snail.

'This snail,' Boris whispered, 'is beyond understanding, beyond undersitting – beyond all human comprehension.'

'Oh good!' said Lavender.

33

'If you wish upon the snail, your wish will surely come true. But take care! For it is dangerous indeed to meddle in magic that you do not understand. The Holy Snail is really only suitable to be used by a trained witch or wizard. What are your magical qualifications, little girl?'

'Um . . . I have a pointy hat?' said Lavender.

'Well then, I'm sure you'll be just fine,' said Boris. 'Would you like it gift-wrapped?'

'Oh yes, please!' Lavender replied.

So Doris whisked the box away, scuttled off, and disappeared once again through the trapdoor.

'Boris, how can I ever thank you?' said Lavender. 'Would you like me to sing you a thank you song?'

'Never!' said Boris.

'It's really no trouble at all,' said Lavender, smiling brightly.

> *'Now I've found the magic spell*
> *I probably won't fall down a well*
> *Or if I do, then I'll just yell . . .'*

'Horace! Doris!' Boris shrieked. 'Come back!! Quickly!!!'

A moment later, Horace appeared, holding a small package, wrapped up in pink paper. Smiling giddily, she leaped over the rabbits, and then curtsied as she put it into Lavender's hands.

'Be careful how you use the Holy Snail, for its powers are great indeed,' said Boris. 'The magic within it is dark and highly dangerous! It can move mountains! It can ruin lives! Also, you need to feed it green leaves, three times a day. Now begone, child, begone!'

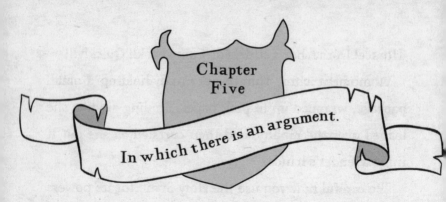

Chapter Five

In which there is an argument.

As Lavender skipped off home, with the Holy Snail safe in her pocket, Boris turned to her weird sisters. 'That was exhausting,' she said. 'Doris, fetch the moonshine, would you?'

She put her feet up on the table, and tossed her pointy hat on to the floor. 'Can one of you go and get the real Holy Snail? All this pretend magic is putting me in the mood for some *actual* magic.'

'Of course, Boris,' said Doris.

She skittered off, and was back a moment later, frowning. 'Um. I'm not sure how to put this,' said Doris. 'But the Holy Snail is . . . Well, it's . . . it's . . .'

'What?' said Boris.

'It's . . . What's the word?'

'What is the word?' said Boris. 'Happy? Asleep? Snail-shaped?'

'It's . . . gone,' said Doris.

'Gone?' said Boris. 'What do you mean, gone?'

'Er . . . it's not there,' said Doris.

Boris gripped the arms of her chair. She took a deep breath. 'After you took the Holy Snail out, to wrap it up, which of you swapped the real Holy Snail for the ordinary snail?' she asked.

'I did,' said Doris and Horace together.

'Excuse me?'

'I did,' Doris and Horace both said again.

Boris looked at Doris. Then she looked at Horace. Who looked back at Doris. Who then turned to Boris. Who had a horrible, sinking feeling. The last time she'd had such a sinking feeling was when she'd been trapped in The Marsh of Unusual Smells.

Terrible as that moment had been, it wasn't half as bad as this one.

'I think,' said Doris, 'there could have been a slight muddle, snail-wise. I think maybe Horace made a small mistake—'

'Actually,' said Horace, 'I think that Doris, maybe, purely by accident – and obviously completely unintentionally – could have made a teeny, tiny error . . .'

'Um, no,' said Doris, 'I'm pretty sure it was Horace.'

'Are you trying to tell me,' said Boris, 'that that child has just taken, from this place, the source of all our magic, the most powerful object in Squerb, the HOLY SNAIL, in exchange for a red button, a silver coin and a small square of something that may have once been fudge?'

'Well, that's not quite true,' said Doris quietly.

'Thank ghouls for that,' said Boris.

'The coin isn't silver,' said Doris. 'I'm pretty sure it's a chocolate coin.' She picked it up, and took a bite, just to check. 'Yep, it's definitely chocolate. Ooh, it's quite good actually.'

Boris knew she had to control her anger. If she let it get the better of her, the same thing always happened. She always turned the thing she was angry with into a rabbit. So it was very important that she remained completely calm.

Stay calm, Boris thought to herself. *Do not raise your voice. Do not lose your temper. DO NOT PANIC. Just count down from one hundred, very slowly.*

One hundred.

Ninety-nine.

Ninety-eight.

'ARGH!' she shrieked. 'The snail! The snail! We must fetch the snail! Fetch the broomsticks! NOW!!!'

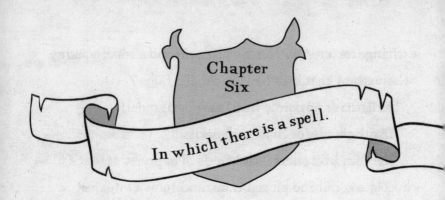

Chapter Six

In which there is a spell.

'Hello, Holy Snail,' Lavender whispered. By now Lavender was back at home, tucked up in bed. Eliza was in her own bed, snoring loudly, and occasionally mumbling, 'Take that, Vorpel!' in her sleep. And, lying at the end of Eliza's bed, Gertrude was quietly gazing up at the moon.

Perhaps Gertrude was thinking poetic thoughts, about the deep, velvety blue of the sky. Or perhaps she was thinking poetic thoughts about the deep, velvety blue of Bonnet's bonnet, which she was eating. It was hard to tell.

As Eliza snored and Gertrude munched, Lavender opened the little box, picked up the snail and held it in her hands. 'Here's some lettuce for you, O Holy Snail,' she said. 'You might not look magical. But I am sure you are.'

'Oh, but of course I am,' the snail replied calmly. 'Why else would I be called the Holy Snail?'

'That's a good point,' said Lavender.

'By the way, that's not my real name,' said the snail.

'Oh,' said Lavender.

'Do you want to know my snail name?'

'Of course!' said Lavender.

'It's Sibooshswhoooshagooshatolipip.'

'Oh. I see. Sibooshswhoooshagooshatolipip?'

'Very good,' said Sibooshswhoooshagooshatolipip. 'But you can call me Sybil if you like.'

'Um, I think that might work better,' said Lavender.

Then the snail looked up at Lavender with her large unblinking eyes. 'Well, what is your first wish?' she said.

'My first wish?'

'First of three. You see, you saved me from Boris, Doris and Horace. They were a nightmare! Constantly bickering. And so many rabbits! Have you ever seen so many rabbits in such a small space? That lot were a fate worse than a flock of blackbirds, I can tell you.'

'I see. Are blackbirds bad?' said Lavender.

Sybil fixed her with a strange stare. Lavender had clearly said something wrong.

'Please go on,' said Lavender. 'You were just telling me about the wishes.'

'Yes,' said Sybil. 'I will grant you three wishes. You can wish for anything at all. You just have to say the magic words: "I wish." And it's best to keep your wish completely secret.'

'I can wish for anything?' Lavender asked.

'Oh yes!' said Sybil. 'Some people say "Be careful what you wish for". But I say, *don't* be careful what you wish for. Which is much more fun.'

And then, to Lavender's delight, Sybil began to sing.

> '*Just make a wish*
> *Don't stop to think,*
> *Just follow, follow your dreams*
> *Just make a wish*
> *For you're on the brink*

Of magical wonderful things!
Wish for a prince or a four-legged fish
Wish for an antelope served on a dish
A Venomous Vorpel that you can vanquish
A centipede wearing a skirt that goes "swish!"
Just wish wish wish wish wish!' *

'Well,' said Sybil. 'Are you ready? I am completely at your surplice.**'

'Oh yes,' said Lavender. 'Here is my first wish: I wish to be tiny, so I can go to a faraway kingdom and fall in love with a tiny prince, and—'

'Your wish is my cummerbund!' said Sybil. There was a flash, and a very loud bang – and Sybil shrank back into her shell.

'Er, Sybil?' Lavender asked. 'Hello? Um . . . Do you know when my wish will come true? Within one to three working

* The Holy Snail is in no way responsible for any injury or death that results from the granting of wishes. Terms and conditions apply.
** Due to Sybil's bad memory, she sometimes gets a few words muddled up.

days? More? And, um, can the prince be as handsome as Prince Magnus the Magnetic?'

But Sybil did not reply. She did not make any noise at all. At least, no noise that a human ear could hear. But if you were a dolphin, a leaf-nosed bat or a ruffed lemur (all animals with a high level of natural magic), you might have heard a strange whine that went:

Oooooffff gugugugug

and

brinnnsnickle

and

shshshwhisshhhhhhhhhhhwhooooshhhhhh . . .

Under Lavender's pillow, the box glowed with a mysterious shimmering light. That was because a glow-worm had ended up inside the box. Then Sybil ate it. Then all was dark.

Chapter Seven

In which nothing strange happens at all.

Outside the farm, the night was dark, and all was still, when several owls suddenly began to hoot, and you might well think that something strange and spooky was about to happen. But that's just because you don't speak owl, so you don't know that they were only saying:

Ooh, I shouldn't have had that second hedgehog. Ooh, too many spines!

Oh, Albert. Again? Every time I get hedgehogs in. And we were going to go for a nice fly around the forest.

Well, I can't move. I'm going to have a nap.

A nap? It's the middle of the night! Honestly. Fat lot of good you are.

So, as you can see, nothing spooky was going on at all. Everything was completely normal.

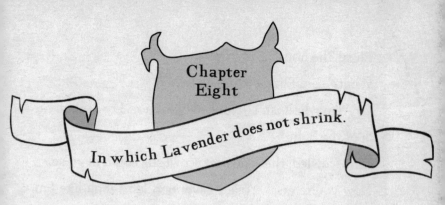

Chapter Eight

In which Lavender does not shrink.

Lying in bed, Lavender couldn't sleep. Of course she couldn't. She'd never met a magical talking snail before. She'd never made a wish to become tiny before. She lay in bed and waited for something to happen. Would it happen all at once, in a moment? Would she suddenly shrink to the size of a thimble, just like that? Or would it happen in stages? Would her ears shrink first? And then her nose? Or would the shrinking start with her toes? Would she shrink from left to right? It was all quite exciting, and she couldn't wait to get started.

'Eliza. Eliza!' she hissed. She hopped out of bed, went over to Eliza, and poked her.

'Put the Vorpel down,' Eliza said sleepily.

'Eliza! The house is on fire!'

'What?' said Eliza, sitting up in bed.

'Or . . . maybe it isn't. It looked like it was. For a moment. Trick of the light.'

Eliza scowled, the scowliest scowl she could manage.

'Now you're awake,' said Lavender, 'do I look like I'm shrinking?'

'No. You look like you're annoying,' said Eliza, still frowning. 'Go back to sleep.'

So Lavender tried to go to sleep, for at least ten seconds. Then she went and knocked on the bathroom door.

'Bonnet. Bonnet?' Lavender whispered, poking her head round the door. 'Do I look like I'm shrinking?'

'What?'

'Do I look to you like I'm shrinking?'

Bonnet frowned. He hadn't been asleep. He was lying in the bath (where he always slept), silently going through his list of worries.

He had been on Worry no. 132: *What if the sky falls in?* He was about to get to Worry no. 133: *What if the sky falls out?*

'No, you don't look like you're shrinking,' said Bonnet.

But he secretly added a whole new worry to his list. Worry no. 3,175: *Is Lavender shrinking?*

Bonnet didn't have much time to dwell on that, and neither did Lavender. Because at that moment, the floor moved.

'Did you feel that?' said Lavender.

'What, that terrifying judder? No, I didn't feel a thing,' said Bonnet. He found the best thing to do, when faced with something strange and scary, was to pretend it hadn't happened.

Then the whole room tilted violently to one side.

'YAAARRRGGGGGH!' yelped Bonnet.

'OOOOOOOHHHH!' said Lavender.

'ARGHH!' shouted Eliza, from her bed.

'Hrmph,' shrugged Gertrude.

Then there was a creak, and a wrenching sound – and everything tilted back the other way. It was as if the house was suddenly adrift on the high seas, in the middle of a terrible storm.

'This must just be a bad dream,' moaned Bonnet, gripping the sides of the bath.

'I don't think it is!' said Lavender. 'Because I only ever have two dreams. In one of them, I marry a prince. And in the other one, I'm singing a song in front of the whole village when I realize that I'm not wearing any pants! And this isn't either of them!'

'HELPPPPP!' yelled Eliza. 'We have to get out! Come on! To the front door!'

So, tripping, sliding and falling, as the floor lurched one way and then the other, they all managed to scramble their way to the kitchen. Now it felt as if the room was zooming upward. Which was clearly impossible. Eliza wondered for one brief, crazy moment, if Grandma Maud was right. Was this The End of the World?

'Come on!' Eliza shouted. 'Follow me! Lavender! Bonnet! Gertrude!' She crawled along the floor as the room trembled and creaked, and swayed from side to side, until finally she got to the door, reached up, grabbed the handle and pulled it open.

'We'll be safer in the garden – let's . . . Yurgh-hargghrukchaaa!' she gasped, which is the noise, it turns out, that some people make when moving swiftly towards a door and then deciding, at the very last moment, not to go through it.

Because, outside the door, the garden simply wasn't there.

Well, that's not quite true.

When Eliza opened the door, she could *see* the garden. It was just quite a long way down. Between Eliza and the garden were several clouds, a pair of owls, and quite a lot of sky.

Then Eliza looked up. Suddenly, everything got a lot scarier. And also, a lot hairier.

'Oh,' said Eliza. Perhaps she should have said something dramatic like 'JACKOW!' or 'By the Great Gizzards of Twimpletroob!' But she hadn't heard of the Great Gizzards of Twimpletroob, so she couldn't say that. And 'Jackow' isn't even a word, so she couldn't say that either. So she simply said 'Oh'.

The last jolt of the house had sent Lavender tumbling towards her sister. Now they were both standing in the doorway, and looking up.

'It's a giant!!' said Lavender.

It was, indeed, a giant. This giant:

By the light of the moon, they could see his great, grim face. His huge bristling eyebrows and his massive jaw. His wild hair that tumbled down to great broad shoulders. His massive arms that were thicker than tree trunks – and looked considerably less friendly.

The giant was holding their house in his hands as he stomped through the fields and forests of Squerb. Wherever he was taking them, it seemed like he was in a hurry.

While Eliza stared, totally speechless, Lavender beamed. 'I always wanted to move house!' she said.

As the giant took another great, thunking step forward, Eliza slammed the front door shut.

'Bonnet,' she said, as the house tilted again, 'you weren't expecting a visitor, were you?'

'Why?' said Bonnet.

'Well, our house is being stolen by a giant!'

'A pirate?' said Bonnet.

'A giant!' shouted Eliza.

'A pastry chef?' said Bonnet.

'A GIANT!' shouted Eliza. 'Our house is being stolen by a GIANT!'

Bonnet was really hoping that he had heard Eliza wrong. Despite being, technically, a giant himself, Bonnet was so scared of giants that he didn't even include them on his lists of fears or worries. It had only been through a series of lucky accidents that Bonnet had ended up in the human world. When he did, he had made a firm decision never to even *think* about giants again.

As the room heeled to the right, Eliza and Lavender slid to the far wall, landing in a pile of pots and pans. It's hard to think when you're covered in saucepans, and Eliza made a mental note to try and avoid it in future.

'How can we stop him, Bonnet?' Eliza yelled. 'Aren't you the giant expert?'

But Bonnet wasn't really in a state to answer her. He would have liked to have given Eliza some really useful giant advice. Unfortunately he was unable to as, at that moment, he did the bravest thing that he could think of:

He fainted.

The giant stomped on through the countryside, their house cradled in his hands.

Fwhomp.

Fwhomp.

Fwhomp.

While Lavender beamed, Eliza panicked and Bonnet lay unconscious on the floor, Gertrude stood, perfectly balanced, on the back of a chair. For the first time in a long time, Gertrude almost had a smile on her face. She even did a little dance.

Of course, Gertrude knew that she was superior to humans in every way. But it was nice to have it demonstrated so clearly.

'We have to do something!' Eliza said, once she had untangled herself from the pile of pots and pans. She scrambled over to the door, leaned out, and shouted upward:

'Oi!! Hey! You! What do you think you're doing?'

The giant took no notice of her.

'Oi!' she shouted. 'Put us down, you massive meanie!'

Then she took aim with her bow and arrow. 'Stop, or I'll shoot!'

When the giant took no notice, Eliza aimed and fired.

Pswoosh! Fwoosh! Shwoosh!

One arrow flew past the giant's face. The second pierced his ear, and just hung there, like a jaunty earring. The third flew up his nose and disappeared. But he completely ignored her. So Eliza ducked back into the room, grabbed all the pots and pans she could find, and flung the door open again.

'Hey!' Eliza yelled. 'Can you stop stealing our house, please?'

She hurled all of the pots and pans at the giant – which

did, finally, get his attention. He looked down, saw Eliza, and chuckled.

'There you are!' he boomed, lifting the house up, so he could get a good look at her. He smiled.

'Hello, teeny-tiny! My name is Too Big. And you are . . . ?'

'I'm Eliza,' said Eliza, suddenly very, very scared.

'You're not Eliza,' said Too Big, with a grin. 'You are MINE. Now back you go into your teeny-tiny house!'

Eliza gasped as he reached forward and picked up her up between finger and thumb, took a good look at her, then posted her back into the house down the chimney.

Fwhomp.

Fwhomp.

Fwhomp.

Too Big strode onward.

Inside the house, Eliza lay, dazed, in the fireplace. Something had happened. Something bad, involving her home. But she couldn't quite remember what it was . . . Had Lavender started filling their bedroom with frogs because she was trying to find the Frog Prince again? Or had she cut the legs off all the chairs so their house could be more like the dwarfs' cottage in *Snow White*?

Then Lavender shrieked, and Eliza was suddenly awake.

'Ooh – the beanstalk! We're going up the beanstalk! Isn't that exciting? What a beautiful morning!' said Lavender, clapping her hands.

As Eliza dragged

herself from the fireplace and looked out of the window, she saw that, unfortunately, her sister appeared to be right.

It *was* a beautiful morning. The sun had risen, and was now shining down on the realm of Squerb, which was slipping further and further away from them with every passing moment. It was also shining down on Too Big the giant, as he climbed an enormous beanstalk that reached up into the clouds.

Chapter Ten

In which there are good manners.

'You go first. No, no, no, please, you go first,' and, 'No, after you, really!' are just a few of the things that giants don't usually say as they clamber up and down the beanstalk that leads up to the Land of the Giants. More often, the giants grunt, step on each other's feet, prise each other's gnarly fingers off the beanstalk, and throw each other out into the huge, empty sky, grarfing.*

But with this particular giant, the other giants really *did* stop. They really *did* say, 'Oh, sorry. Let me get out of your way. Do you need me to jump off the beanstalk? Yes? No trouble at all. Oh, it's only a mile or two down. My pleasure!'

* A giant word for 'grunting and laughing'.

Too Big just seemed to have that effect on other giants.

So, very soon, Too Big had climbed all the way up to the top of the beanstalk, where he hauled himself up on to the cliffs, stopped for a moment, and then grarfed with satisfaction.

They had reached the Land of the Giants.

Inside the little wooden box in Lavender's pocket, the Holy Snail fizzed gently with excitement. She allowed herself to eat another leaf, because her strange magic was working. It was  wonderful, granting wishes! So unpredictable! So magical! So fulfilling. It almost always worked wonderfully.* Who knew what would happen next?

*

---

* Actually, it almost always worked abysmally. And it usually ended in tears.

But wait.

HALT!

BE STILL.

Whatever happened to Boris and her weird sisters? Were they hot on the heels of the giant? Well, no. Not really. They weren't even slightly warm on the heels of the giant.

For although Boris, Doris and Horace had set out to find Lavender and the snail as fast as they could, unfortunately for them, that wasn't very fast at all.

First, Doris had taken four hours to decide which cape would go best with her broomstick. Then she had taken another two hours to work out which gloves would go best with her cape. Then Horace had forgotten her hat, and had to go back for it. Finally Boris had got so angry with Horace and Doris that she needed to spend several hours alone, calmly counting down from one hundred, before they could set off.

At last, they were zooming over the The Marsh of Unusual Smells on their broomsticks, at full speed – 2.7 miles an hour.

'Oooh – isn't it a thrill?' said Doris. 'I love quests!'

Isn't that just typical of Doris? thought Boris. *She simply has no idea of the gravity of the situation.*

But it turned out that none of the witches had much idea of the gravity of the situation. For at that precise moment all the magic in their broomsticks ran out. There was a rackety, spluttering sound, then there was no sound at all . . . and then they all fell headlong into the marsh.

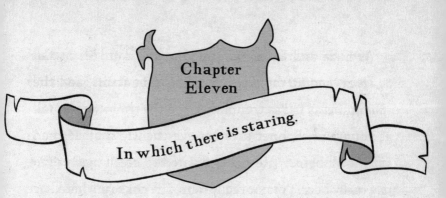

Chapter Eleven

In which there is staring.

Lavender stared. Eliza stared. Gertrude nibbled quietly on a sock. As Too Big strode along, they were all speechless. Because this was it. The Land of the Giants. The whole place seemed to be covered by thick forest. And nothing in the forest was small. (Apart from the whales. Whales here were tiny, for some reason, and eked out a meagre existence at the bottom of puddles.)

Actual size

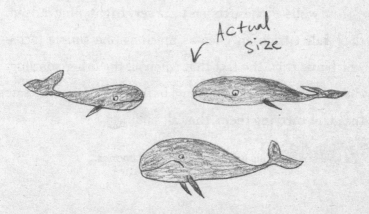

As Eliza and Lavender stared at the daffodils as tall as trees, and at the trees as tall as mountains, and the mountains as tall as trountains, and the trountains as tall as zountains, Bonnet kept his eyes tightly shut. He had seen it all before. He never wanted to see it again. 'I'm not really here, I'm not really here, I'm not really here,' he muttered to himself.

What Bonnet *really* didn't want to look at were the giants. There were giants grinning as they headbutted each other. There were giants singing around open fires, as they shovelled whole hogs into their mouths. There were giants bashing each other over the head with enormous clubs, and dancing in enormous clubs, and playing cards with enormous clubs.*

And while all these things were very frightening indeed, they didn't frighten Eliza as much as one simple fact – which was this. The fact that when all the other snarling, club-wielding, cow-swallowing, buffalo-tossing giants saw the giant carrying them, they all said:

* As well as enormous hearts, spades and diamonds.

'*Good day, Too Big!*' and

'*Morning, Mr T!*' and

'*Arghhh – it's Too Big – run!!!*'

'He's not just a giant,' gulped Eliza. 'He's the giant that even giants are frightened of.'

'Ooh – look at that beautiful flower!' said Lavender, pointing to an enormous orange flower.

'It's so big, I could live in it, like Thumbelina,' she said. And then her eyes went wide and her heart began to beat and her brain went *fwhisshwhooshping!* as she remembered her magical wish:

I wish to be tiny, so I can go to a faraway kingdom . . .

Wait. Hold on. No! Yes! What?

Lavender's mind was really spinning now. Spinning faster and faster. If there had been any socks inside her mind, they would have been completely dry.

Has the snail's magic begun to work? she wondered. 'But that's incredible!' she shouted.

'What's incredible?' said Eliza.

'Um, nothing,' said Lavender. She wanted to tell her

sister everything. But Sybil had told her to keep her wish a secret. So she didn't say anything to Eliza. Instead, she contented herself with singing a little song.

> '*Some say that it's diamonds,*
> *Some say that it's boys,*
> *Some say that it's unicorns*
> *Or bicycles or toys.*
>
> *But I have found the answer,*
> *On that you can depend.*
> *Snails, snails, snails*
> *Are a girl's best friend.*'

Then, when no one was looking, she got the wooden box out of her pocket.

'Sybil!' she whispered. 'Is this all your magical doing?'

'Of course it is,' whispered Sybil. 'You are at the start of the most incredible denture.* You just have to let it unfold.'

---

* Sybil did get her words muddled up quite often. But you have to remember that her entire brain was only about 2mm wide.

'I do?'

'Really, there's nothing to worry about,' said Sybil calmly. 'I'm completely rustworthy, I promise you. Hand on heart.*'

'Oh. Excellent!'

'You know what they say: snails are all you need!**'

'Definitely!'

'And whatever you've heard about any mistakes I may have made in the past – that was all probably made up by a jealous centipede.***'

'Er, what was that?' asked Lavender. But by now, Sybil had shrunk back into her shell. So Lavender shut the box,

---

* This might have been a more convincing promise if Sybil actually had a hand.

** They don't say that.

*** In the past, Sybil's magic may have gone wrong. Just once or twice. It's just possible, for example, that a girl who wished to live at the bottom of the sea, as a mermaid, ended up at the bottom of the sea, as a barmaid. And that a man who wished he could fly, ended up just being able to lie. On the floor. Which had never been that hard for him anyway. Oh, and one old lady who wanted a talking cat . . . got a talking mat. Actually, that one wasn't really Sybil's fault. It just turned out that the mat was incredibly annoying. Luckily for Sybil, she had quite a short memory, so she wasn't too troubled by any of this.

and put it back in her pocket. 'It's all going to be fine!' she said. 'We're all going on a magical adventure!'

'What?' said Eliza, who had been staring out of the window. 'Have you gone mad?'

'No!' said Lavender. 'I just think that everything's quite exciting!'

'This is *not* exciting!' said Eliza. 'And this is not an adventure, this is a disaster! Because we are very, very far from home, and we'll probably get eaten, and – oh no! OH NO! Grandma Maud!' she cried. 'She'll come back home, and we'll just have – disappeared! The house will be gone!'

'Oh really, Eliza, Grandma will be fine,' said Lavender.

'Why would she be fine?' said Eliza. 'You've gone soft in the head! Was your brain replaced by a flan in the night? Was it stolen by a Vorpel in your sleep? Did you swap brains with a pigeon overnight?'

'No,' said Lavender. 'I'm simply enjoying this exciting opportunity to see the world. Who knows what might happen?!'

'*I* know what might happen!' Eliza replied. 'And I

know it's not going to be good!'

'Oh Eliza,' said Lavender. 'You're so negative. Look at that! You don't see something like that every day.'

It was true, thought Eliza. *You didn't see something like that every day.* They had come to a halt in front of a rock face. A very stern rock face.

The rock face was etched on to a massive boulder, which Too Big picked up and tossed to one side, as easily as if it was a toothpick. He stepped into the hole behind it.

'That's it,' said Eliza, as they were plunged into darkness. 'He's really got us now.'

FWHOMP.

Too Big plonked the house down on the floor.

Eliza stared out of the window as her eyes adjusted to the darkness of the cave. In the middle of the cave, she could see a big, crackling bonfire. The flames lit up a collection of strange objects that were hanging on the walls. One wall was devoted to axes and clubs.

Another wall was covered in shining, silver trophies.

And hanging from the ceiling, on a series of long, brown ropes, were some even more frightening objects: swords, harpoons and lances.

'Where are we?' she gasped.

'We're nowhere,' said Bonnet, who still had his eyes shut tight. 'I'm not here. You're not here. This never happened.'

'We are here,' said Eliza. 'And we have to – Hey! What happened? Why did everything go dark?'

Suddenly Eliza couldn't see a thing. The house was jiggling and rolling around again. Then, very close by, Too Big's deep, booming voice said: 'Silence, my teeny-tinies! I don't want to ruin the surprise.'

The surprise? What was the surprise? Whatever it was, Eliza thought it was unlikely to be good.

'We've got to get out of here!' Eliza whispered.

She felt her way to the kitchen door and opened it. But when she tried to walk through it, she went head first into something *furry*. Something that was stretched over the doorway.

'Bonnet! Lavender! Gertrude!' she shouted. 'We're trapped! The giant's trapped us inside the house! We've got to get out!'

But Bonnet wasn't going to risk going anywhere. He was quietly sitting in the corner, reciting his worries to himself.

'Worry no. 72,' he muttered. 'Napkins: Is it true that

they're all having a nap, and one day they're going to wake up, and turn into wake-kins? And what will they do then? Worry no. 73: Spoons. They seem sinister. Why?'

Meanwhile, Lavender was quietly singing a song.

> *'When you're feeling lonely,*
> *Bad or sad or blue*
> *Just look around, upon the ground*
> *At what's in front of you*
> *And if it's been raining*
> *Be careful where you tread*
> *For you don't want to step upon*
> *Your brand new best friend's head*
> *For snails, snails, snails*
> *Snails are the best!'*

And what about Gertrude? Was Gertrude using the darkness to think up a fantastic escape plan? Or was she, in fact, using the darkness to eat another one of Bonnet's bonnets? We'll never know.

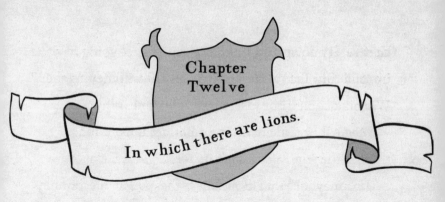

Chapter Twelve

In which there are lions.

As she waited in the darkness, Eliza heard some frightening sounds. First came a rumble of something that sounded like thunder. Then came the sounds of stamping, shrieking, squealing and laughing. *This truly must be The End of the World*, she thought.

Meanwhile, Too Big was feeling quite content as he gazed at his daughter, Chewy. Her birthday party was going like a dream.

'Everybody, settle down,' he said, facing the crowd of giant children inside the cave. 'For now it is time for your favourite game. Sleeping lions!'

'Sleeping lions!' Chewy cried with glee. Then Too Big whistled three times, and three lions came trooping into the cave, lay down and went to sleep.

Inside Old Tumbledown Farm, Eliza was listening.

'I think something just *roared*,' she said.

'Maybe it was the wind,' said Bonnet hopefully.

'Does the wind also gnash its teeth?' said Eliza.

'Um, maybe?' said Bonnet, as he pulled his bonnet down over his head, and pretended he was far, far away.

'Now, children, before we begin, please remember, the most important thing about this game is SAFETY,' Too Big said. 'Do not put your heads inside the lions' mouths, just to see if they fit. You don't want to end up like little Grubber did last year, do you?'

The crowd of giant children all solemnly shook their heads.

'Because that didn't end well, did it?'

They shook their heads again.

'Well then. Three, two, one – go!'

Too Big watched proudly as Chewy and her friends went to bounce up and down on the lions, and ruffle their fur, and make knots in their tails. He chuckled when the lions all woke up and chased them round and round the cave. Finally, Too Big chased the lions away. (His roar, it turned out, was much more frightening than theirs.)

After that, it was time for 'Pass the Bludgeon'. Then it was time for 'Pin the Tail on the Donkey'. Which the giant children loved, although the donkey wasn't quite so thrilled. After the donkey had hobbled out of the cave, it was time for cake.

'Here you go, my little Chew-Chew,' Too Big said proudly. 'I made you a cake with all your favourite things. Buffalo brains, wolves' tails and chicken beaks!'

'Oh thank you, thank you, Daddy!' Chewy cried, clapping her hands. She took a big slice of the red, slimy, crunchy, feathery cake, and soon her face was covered in bright red cake juice. Finally, when her friends Snotty, Bitey, Lumphead, Guzzler, Bonebrain and Knucklehead had all gone home, full of cake, and each carrying their very own axe, it was time for Chewy to open her presents.

Too Big made her shut her eyes. Then he led her over to the back of the cave, and stopped in front of an enormous parcel, all wrapped up in goatskins.

When Chewy saw it, her eyes lit up. As she tore off the goatskins, light flooded back into Old Tumbledown Farm.

'Uh-oh,' said Eliza, looking out through the kitchen window, and spotting the little giantess. She saw Chewy's hair, wild and black, as if a cloud of fighting ravens had all been glued together. Next, she saw her grin, huge and wide, and as comforting as a hug from a shark. Then she saw her bright, excited eyes peering in through the window.

'A DOLL'S HOUSE!' Chewy yelled.

'Happy birthday, my little Chew-Chew!' said Too Big. 'Here it is. A teeny-tiny house, with some real live teeny-tinies, all for you!'

'It's perfect!' shouted Chewy.

'Quick!' Eliza gasped. 'Bonnet! Lavender! Gertrude!

Get into the cupboards! Under the table! Hide!'

But it was too late. Before Eliza had a chance to move, two sticky, goo-covered hands forced their way through the front door.

'Come here, my little dolls!' Chewy cried. She managed to grasp Lavender by her hat, and pull her out of the house. A moment later, she was also holding the wriggling, struggling Eliza.

'Aaaargh!' said Eliza.

'Hello!' said Lavender brightly.

'I am Chewy. I am four years old TODAY!' Chewy said proudly. 'This has been my favourite birthday ever. Today I became your new owner!'

Eliza shivered as Chewy smiled. She looked very happy indeed.

Now, most people agree that happy children are, in general, a good thing. Most people would

prefer to see a happy child than, say, a happy
dictator . . .

or a happy Vorpel.

But there are exceptions to
this rule. One of them is when the
happy child is five metres tall,
and dribbling on you from
above, while gripping you in
her fist, shaking you up and

A happy
Vorpel →

down, and shouting: 'Teeny-tiny!!!' over and over again.

'That's right, my little Chewy,' Too Big said fondly. 'My
special little girl deserves a very special present. These
wonderful dolls will do whatever you say!'

'Oh we will, will we?' said Eliza.

'Yes, you will,' said Too Big, with a grarf. 'If you don't
want to be eaten or squashed.'

Then Too Big smiled down proudly at his daughter,
and ruffled her hair, as Chewy smiled down proudly at her
new 'dolls', and ruffled their hair. Then, putting them
down on the floor of the cave, she crouched down and

took a good look at her new doll's house.

'Oh look, a nice front door!' she said, breaking the door off. 'And here is the chimney!' she said. 'Oh – that was the chimney. It broke itself on my hand. And look, there's another one!'

Through the window, Chewy had spied Bonnet. He was lying fully clothed in the bath, with his eyes shut, and his bonnet over his head, mumbling 'None of this is happening', over and over again.

'Funny little round doll!' she said, as she reached in through the window and picked Bonnet up by his feet.

'Hello!' she said, plonking him down next to Eliza and Lavender. 'And look – a little pony!'

'Ah, no,' said Too Big wisely. 'That's not a pony. That is a *mouse*. Now he's your pet.'

Chewy picked up the disgruntled Gertrude by the scruff of her neck, and held her up to get a good look at her. But Gertrude wasn't having any of it. She twisted her head around and bit Chewy as hard she could on the thumb.

'Oooh! The little mousey is tickling me!' Chewy giggled as she plonked Gertrude down next to the others.

'Funny little dolls!' Chewy said.

'Actually, we're not dolls,' said Eliza. 'We're people. From Squerb. And we'd quite like to go home now, if that's all right.'

'No, no, no,' said Chewy, frowning now. 'You belong to me. Daddy got you from the shop. Didn't you, Daddy?'

'I did,' boomed Too Big.

'The shop?!' said Eliza. 'We didn't come from a shop! We came from Squerb!'

'*You* might call it Squerb,' roared Too Big. 'We call it "the shop". Although some giants call it "the larder". We can call it that, if that will make you happy?'

'No!' said Eliza.

'The toy shop?'

'No!'

'The miniature zoo?'

'No!'

'The enormous toilet?'

'No!!!' said Eliza.

'Suit yourself,' said Too Big.

'The point is,' said Eliza, 'you can't just buy people and then give them away as presents!'

'That is true,' said Too Big. 'You are quite smart for someone with such a teeny-tiny brain. But I didn't buy you. I didn't pay any money for you at all. You were all free gifts!'

'But, but – you can't just steal people, and their homes!' said Eliza.

'Ah, no,' said Too Big, with a friendly smile. 'I was not stealing, I was "taking". Taking is completely different to stealing.'

'How?'

'Well, they are spelled *completely differently*.'

'But . . . but . . . but that isn't fair!' said Eliza.

'Fair?' said Too Big. 'What does this word, "fair", mean?

Ah – I know! It is one of those places with rides and apple-bobbing.'

'No,' said Eliza. 'Fair, as in good. And true, and right.'

Too Big scratched his head. 'Nope. Never heard of it,' he said, with a shrug. 'Oh well.'

Eliza glared at him, and tried to look as fierce as possible. 'We demand that you take us HOME,' she said.

'You know,' said Too Big, 'you really do not want to argue with me. I am Too Big, Too Big To Fail! I am famous throughout the Land of the Giants. I am the Champion of Oxen Tossing! Of Tree Crunching! Of Axe Hurling! Of Octopus Wrestling! Of Boulder Smashing! Of Shark Juggling! Of Fire Farting! So you will be good little dolls for my lovely daughter.'

'Or what?' said Eliza.

'Or you will become nibbles,' growled Too Big.

'*Nibbles?* Nibbles for who?' Eliza asked.

'Nibbles for Nibbles, of course!' Too Big said. 'Come here, Nibbles.'

Eliza gulped, Bonnet swayed, and Gertrude tried very hard not to tremble, as an enormous, ginger beast appeared, padding across the floor towards Too Big.

Nibbles →

size of
ordinary
cat ↓

'Here, Nibbles,' said Too Big fondly, stroking the clawed monster that was now purring and nuzzling his legs. Eliza scowled at the beast. The beast hissed back.

'She likes her nibbles, does Nibbles,' Too Big said.

'Especially tasty little mice!' Chewy said, bouncing up and down with excitement. 'Nibbles loves playing Cat and Mouse!'

Hearing this, Gertrude clomped her hooves on the ground. She stood on one leg. She bleated. In general, she tried to look as goat-like as possible.

'Funny little dancing mouse!' Chewy cried. 'Nibbles will love playing with you!'

'Now,' Too Big continued. 'You must all be good. Do not try to escape. And do not make Chewy upset. If you do, Too Big will crush you.'

'Crush us like what?' said Eliza, still trying to be defiant.

'Too Big will crush you,' said Too Big, 'like the teeny-tiny, easily squashable humans that you are.'

'Oh,' said Eliza. 'Right.'

With that, Too Big left Chewy to play with her new

dolls. Now they had a menacing, gigantic beast staring at them, and a menacing, gigantic giant threatening to squash them, they weren't about to disobey their orders. So they did exactly what Chewy wanted them to do.

When Chewy tried to use Bonnet as a yo-yo, he went along with it.

'This is so much fun!' he managed to say, as he turned white and was sick into his own bonnet.

When Chewy got Eliza to dress up as a princess, and sing a song about how much she loved rainbows and daisies, Eliza did exactly that. When Chewy told Gertrude to dance, Gertrude danced. When she made them all eat her birthday cake, they all tucked into it.

'Mmmmn,' said Bonnet. 'You can really taste the wolves' tails, can't you? Very . . . flavoursome.'

And when she told Lavender to sing . . . of course, Lavender sang.

'Your songs are so grimbly!' said Chewy, gurgling with laughter. Luckily for everyone, Lavender didn't know that 'grimbly' was a giant word that means 'so bad it's good'.

At least Chewy's happy, Eliza thought. That meant that Too Big wouldn't squash them quite yet. Which had to be a good thing. Didn't it?

'You are my favourite ever presents!' Chewy told them. 'I am going to keep you FOREVER!'

Oh. Right.

'Hooray!' said Eliza, weakly. 'That's just . . . perfect.'

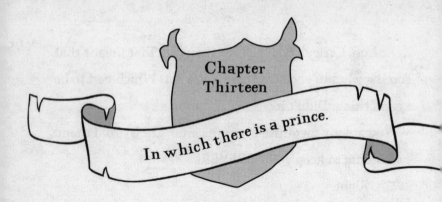

Chapter Thirteen

In which there is a prince.

At long last, there was a moment of peace, as Chewy put down her 'dolls' for a moment, to unwrap another birthday present.

'Eliza,' Lavender whispered. 'I really should tell you something.'

'What?' said Eliza.

'Um,' said Lavender. 'Well . . . I suppose. You see. This all began . . .'

'What all began?'

Lavender hesitated. She wasn't quite sure how to tell her sister about the Holy Snail, and her magical wish. But she had a horrible, nagging feeling that she should. While Lavender tried to work out what to say,

Chewy unwrapped another parcel.

'A tiny little carriage!' Chewy cried.

As she put it down on the ground, the carriage door burst open, and a man jumped out.

'Look at that!' said Chewy. 'Another walking, talking doll!'

'What did you want to tell me?' Eliza asked her sister.

'My prince . . .' breathed Lavender, gazing at the man who had just stepped out of the carriage. He was dressed in a blue silk suit, and wore black shoes with golden buckles. At his side was a golden sword, around his neck was a large golden ruff, on his face was a small pair of gold spectacles, and on his head was a golden crown.

Of all the princes in Lavender's imagination, none was quite so princely as the man she now saw before her, blinking and looking around with a slightly dazed expression on his face.

If he was surprised to find himself in a cave, staring up at a smiling, dribbling giant, he quickly decided to hide it.

'Ah. Good afternoon,' he said to Chewy. 'A pleasure to

meet you. You must be Mrs Bumbletrout, the Mayor of Little Wimbling.'

'You are a funny little doll,' said Chewy, smiling.

'I am Prince Ludwig von Flonderfling,' he said, with a bow. 'Allow me to present you with a small token of friendship, a portrait of my great-great-grandmother, Queen Wilhelmina.'

'Another present!' said Chewy. As the prince held out the portrait, she plucked it from his fingers, and ate it.

'It's crunchy!' she said, delighted.

'Well, yes. Quite,' said Prince Ludwig. The important thing about royal visits, he knew, was to smile and be polite, whatever happened.

'What a charming town you have here, Mrs Bumbletrout. Perhaps a little darker than I imagined, but, really, very – well, very characterful . . .'

At this point Chewy picked up the prince, to get a good look at him.

'Nice little talking doll!' said Chewy.

The prince paused for a moment as she dangled him

between her thumb and finger. For the first time it occurred to him that there might be something wrong with this royal visit.

'Now you will dance!' said Chewy, putting the prince down next to her other dolls. 'Or I will feed you to Nibbles!'

'Ha ha, I'm sure you will,' said the prince politely. He wasn't sure what 'being fed to Nibbles' involved, but it was probably one of those traditional village ceremonies that was quite fun once you got into it.

As she looked on, Eliza felt quite sorry for Prince Ludwig. Clearly, he wasn't the sharpest tool in the box. In fact, of all the tools in the box, sharpness-wise, Prince Ludwig would probably be a sponge.

'You know, you're actually in a cave, in the Land of the Giants,' Eliza whispered.

'Ah, no, I don't think so. I think you'll find that this is Little Wimbling. I'm actually on a very important royal visit. If you don't mind.'

'No, you're in the Land of the Giants,' Eliza explained.

'That's why the small child you're talking to is five metres high.'

'That's where you're wrong,' said Prince Ludwig. 'I would never go to the Land of the Giants. I really don't like the sound of them, those horrid, enormous – Oh. Oh dear.'

The prince was looking at Chewy again.

'I knew there was something odd about her!' he said.

'Mnnn,' said Eliza.

'But she's gargantuan!'

'Yes,' said Eliza.

'She's unnatural!'

'Yes.'

'Monstrous!'

'Yup.'

'Gigantic!'

'Well yes, she's a giant . . .'

'Where's my butler? Godfrey? Godfrey!!' said Prince Ludwig, looking wildly around.

'Um, I think you're on your own,' said Eliza.

'But that's completely out of the question!' said the prince. 'I'm not having it. I'm just not having it. Look here! I am Prince Ludwig von Flonderfling,' he shouted at Chewy. 'If you think for one moment that you can just keep me here, then I'll . . . I'll . . . I'll . . . I'll sing, and I'll dance, and I'll leap with joy at the beauty and the sheer wonder of being alive.'

As threatening speeches went, Prince Ludwig's was not the most effective. Because, halfway through his speech, he looked up, and spotted Lavender.

Lavender, who had been gazing at him ever since he'd stumbled out of his golden carriage.

Lavender, who had been murmuring the words, 'My prince!' over and over again since she'd first seen him.

And as Prince Ludwig set eyes on her, he experienced seven strange sensations, all at once. His heart leaped. His knees trembled. His hands shook. His tongue went dry. His elbows tingled. His mouth fell open like a trapdoor. His mind scrambled like an egg.

'What is your name, fair maiden?' he breathed.

'My Lavender is name,' Lavender said gently. 'I mean, my lame is Navender. Sorry – my *name* is *Lavender*.'

'Navender,' the prince echoed, reverently.

'No, Lavender,' said Lavender. 'I'm Lavender.'

'It is an honour to meet you, Lavender,' said the prince, kneeling before her.

'It *is* an honour to meet me,' said Lavender, trying to be as polite, and princess-like, as possible.

Perhaps I am in a strange, faraway land, Prince Ludwig thought. *Perhaps there is a very large child, dribbling on me from above. Perhaps there is a cat standing behind her that is roughly the same height as my palace, with an expression more savage than that of my great-aunt Bertha before breakfast. But what does that matter? I am in LOVE.*

And as for Lavender, the moment she saw him, she knew that the Holy Snail's spell had worked. Her magical wish had come true!

'Sybil, you've really done it!' she whispered, turning away from the prince for a brief moment.

96

'Of course I have!' Sybil whispered back. 'Honestly, don't look so shell-shocked! For I am, quite simply, the most magical snail you will ever meet. Now, tell me your second wish. Go on!'

'Oh, I don't know,' Lavender whispered. 'What more could I want than this?'

'Well, you'd better get thinking. And by the way, I am getting a little bit peckish . . .'

But Lavender was no longer listening. She slammed the little wooden box shut.

'If I may be so bold,' said Prince Ludwig. 'You are the most beautiful, the most radiant creature that I have ever set eyes on.'

'And you are the most handsome, and the only prince that I have ever set eyes on,' said Lavender.

'Let me guess,' said Prince Ludwig. 'You come from a great city.'

'I do,' said Lavender. 'I come from afar—'

'Um, no, she comes from a *farm*,' interrupted Eliza. 'In Squerb. Not to interrupt or anything, but maybe we could all – you know – think up a plan? To escape from the giants?'

'The giants?' said the prince blankly. Then he looked up and saw the huge, dribbling child, still staring down at him, fascinated. Standing behind her was an even larger, hairier giant who looked like (and in fact was) her father. And curling around his legs was the demonic-looking beast with syrup-coloured eyes called 'Nibbles'.

'*Those* giants,' said Eliza.

'Oh yes, those giants,' echoed Prince Ludwig calmly. 'Oh, I'm sure they don't mean any harm.'

For now Lavender and the prince were in love, it seemed to them both as if nothing else mattered.

'We really need to get out of here!' said Eliza. But before she could come up with a plan, Chewy clapped her hands again.

'More dancing, dolls!' she cried.

Eliza knew better than to disobey her. So they all sang and danced for Chewy.

It was hours and many songs later that Too Big finally

shouted: 'Bedtime, Chewy!' And Chewy put her poor, exhausted dolls away in her doll's house.

'Night night, then. Sleep well, my little dolls!'

Chewy smiled a big, toothy smile at her dolls. And as she shut the door to Old Tumbledown Farm, they all breathed a sigh of relief.

Eliza watched through the window as Chewy ran over to her father. He brushed her hair with a cludgeon . . .*

Then he washed her face with moap . . .**

* A cross between a club and a bludgeon that was used for many things around the cave, including brushing hair, eating and general bashing.
** Moap is a giant's word for soap. It is made from mud and mud.

Finally, he tucked her up in bed.

'Night-night, sleep tight, and if the bedbugs bite . . .'

'Then I'll bite them back,' Chewy said sweetly. 'And then bash them with a club, or biff them on the nose. Or pull them by their ears.'

'Very good,' Too Big said, giving his daughter a goodnight kiss.

Inside Old Tumbledown Farm, Eliza listened carefully, until she heard Chewy snoring (like a rhinoceros) and Too Big snorting (like a rhinoceros with a terrible cold).

'They're asleep!' she hissed to the others. 'Come on! This is our chance! This is our chance to get home!'

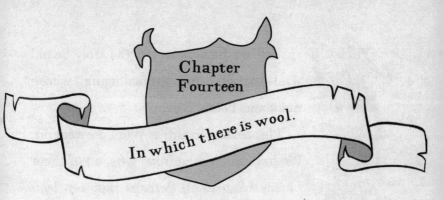

Chapter
Fourteen

In which there is wool.

Meanwhile, what had happened to those weird sisters, Boris, Doris and Horace?

Well, after dragging themselves out of the marsh, they had crept into the Haunted Forest to continue searching for the missing snail.

'Have you seen the Holy Snail?' Boris asked three mysterious figures who appeared on the path before her.

'We have seen the Very Surprising Caterpillar,' said the first mysterious figure.

'And earlier we had a cup of tea with the Enlightened Woodlouse,' said the second mysterious figure.

'And I just stepped on a worm,' said the third mysterious figure.

'But we have not seen the Holy Snail,' said the first mysterious figure, whose name was Peter.

'We are the Wizards of Wool,' he went on. 'We have many wondrous gifts, all of them made from wool. Perhaps they can lead you to this wondrous mollusc. For here is a compass, made of wool . . .'

'And here is a rowing boat made of wool,' said the second wizard.

'And a cucumber sandwich made of wool.'

'Er,' said Boris. 'Thanks, but I think we'll be fine.'

'As you wish,' said Peter, a little sadly. 'You probably don't want our flying carpet either. I'm afraid it is an early model. It doesn't even have a steering wheel.'

'A flying carpet?' said

Boris. 'For that, we would be most grateful.'

'Really?' said Peter. 'It's a bit frayed around the edges.'

'We'd love it,' said Boris, firmly.

And so, from out of one of his very long sleeves, Peter produced a carpet. He laid it on the ground, and as Boris, Doris and Horace stepped on to it, he boomed: 'Flying carpet of wool, to the Holy Snail!'

The carpet zoomed up into the sky.

'Ayyeee!' screamed Horace.

'Arghh!' screamed Doris.

'How did you say the steering worked?' yelled Boris. But now the wizards were far below them, smiling and waving as the witches zoomed off into the sky.

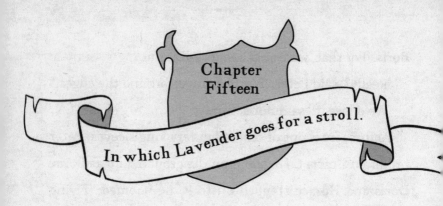

Chapter Fifteen

In which Lavender goes for a stroll.

Back inside the cave, while Too Big was snoring like a champion (which in fact, he was*) . . . Eliza was all set to escape. There were just a couple of tiny problems to deal with first.

'I don't really see what the fuss is all about,' said Lavender. 'Why do you want to leave? This has been the best day of my life!'

'I agree with Labrador,' said the prince, putting a protective arm around her.

'Um, it's Lavender, not Labrador,' said Lavender.

'So sorry, Labrador,' said Prince Ludwig.

---

* He was the current Sleepathon Champion, which involved farting, drooling and snoring all at the same time.

'It's, it's – it's fine,' said Lavender, smiling sweetly at him.

'Lavender, if we stay here, we're going to get EATEN,' Eliza fumed. 'Are you even listening to me?'

'You're right,' said Lavender. 'Prince Ludwig and I *are* perfect for each other.'

Prince Ludwig nodded, and then gave Lavender a smile so gormless that Eliza really wished she had a bottle of gorm handy, so she could throw it right at his head.

'Listen,' said Eliza. 'If we don't get out of here and find the beanstalk, we'll be toast. We'll get squashed by Chewy, or stepped on by Too Big, or swallowed by Nibbles. So come on! Or do I have to go out there on my own?'

'Bonnet will go with you, won't you, Bonnet?' Lavender said.

'I suppose I could come with you,' Bonnet said with a gulp. 'Er . . .'

Eliza turned to Bonnet, who was sitting in the corner of the kitchen, nervously eating scones. He was covered in crumbs from head to foot, and shaking all over.

'Really?' she said.

'Of course,' Bonnet said. 'I'll just, er, get a few things ready first. I'll need to make an expedition map. And an expedition cake. And some expedition socks. And expedition disguises. And expedition umbrellas. And an expedition carriage of some sort. But after that, I'll be completely ready to go.'

'Bonnet?' said Eliza.

'Yes?'

'We have to go now. Tonight.'

'*Tonight* tonight?' said Bonnet.

'Yes, tonight tonight.'

'Not next week, next week?'

'No.'

'In a month, in a month?'

'No.'

'In a year, in a year?'

'TONIGHT. Otherwise we could very easily get EATEN.'

'I see.' Bonnet gulped again. He did see. He saw the fact that outside, in the Land of the Giants, he was going to face at least 137 of his very worst fears. Outside, there were hundreds of giant plants (scary) and thousands of giant animals (terrifying). And that was before he started thinking about the actual giants. The numberless giants. Who were all waiting to terrify him, tread on him, eat him, or all of the above. At least inside the cave there were only *three* terrifying creatures that could kill him at any moment.

'Wait!' said Bonnet. 'I've had an idea!'

It was a blindingly good idea. It was up there with the time that he invented the jam roll.*

'Why don't we just wait here for a little while, just in case all the giants decide to um . . . er . . . leave?'

But he could tell from Eliza's face that she didn't quite understand what a great idea this was.

'Just give me one minute,' he said. 'Because I know that I'm going to think of a brilliant and completely safe way to get everyone home. Without going . . . out there.'

* Bonnet may not have been the first person on earth to eat a jam roll. No, that was Margery Fripperclonk of Lewes, Sussex (985–1022) – also known as Sticky Margery.

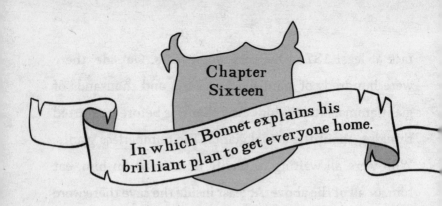

Chapter Sixteen

In which Bonnet explains his brilliant plan to get everyone home.

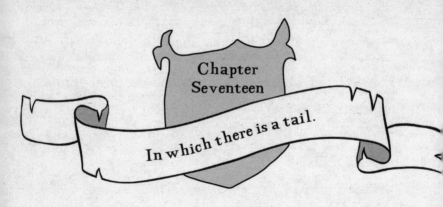

'So?' asked Eliza. 'This brilliant plan?'

'Um . . .' said Bonnet. 'Er . . .'

'Right then,' said Eliza. 'Let's go.'

In the end, Bonnet did all his expedition preparations very quickly. He just turned his face to the wall and let out a long, silent scream.

A few moments later, Eliza, Bonnet and Gertrude crept out of Old Tumbledown Farm, and tiptoed past the sleeping Chewy, and the snoring Too Big, as quietly as they could.

'Wait! Wait for me!' shouted Lavender, just as they were edging past Nibbles, who was curled up just next to the entrance. 'Prince Ludwig and I are coming with you!'

'Yes, wait for us!' Prince Ludwig shouted merrily.

'Shhhhh!' said Eliza, as Lavender and the prince came skipping through the cave hand in hand.

'Why do we need to be quiet?' asked Lavender, as she stepped on Nibbles's tail.

Nibbles opened her yellow eyes and in one swift movement sprang to her feet.

'Oh, what a lovely creature!' said Prince Ludwig, as Nibbles hissed and bared her teeth. Then she crouched down, and launched herself at the nearest edible-looking creature – which happened to be Gertrude.

'Gargh!' Gertrude cried, leaping into the air. Nibbles missed her by a whisker. She snarled.

'Hey!' shouted Eliza. 'You great big brute! Take that!'

Eliza fired an arrow at Nibbles, and then another, but Nibbles quite literally shrugged them off.

'Run!' Eliza screamed.

So Gertrude ran for her life, and Bonnet ran for his life. Bonnet made it out of the cave, but Gertrude was not so lucky. Unfortunately Gertrude was so panicked that she just ran round and round in circles.

'Outside, Gertrude – OUTSIDE!' Eliza yelled. But it made no difference. Gertrude kept running until she was as dizzy as a squid in a seafood-hurling contest.

Finally Gertrude did stop running, but only so she could fall over. When she looked up, she found herself staring at the large, ginger face of Nibbles.

Nibbles licked her lips. She crouched down. She sprang forward – just as Prince Ludwig and Lavender strolled past.

Now, Lavender and Prince Ludwig were not, at this stage, taking any notice of Gertrude's Imminent Death. They were gazing deep into each other's eyes. As they gazed, Prince Ludwig walked straight into an enormous cludgeon, which toppled over and landed on Nibbles's tail.

'YEOUW!!!' Nibbles screeched, leaping into the air.

She hissed and whirled around, to find out what savage beast had attacked her. Meanwhile Eliza and Gertrude ran for their lives. This time, Gertrude managed to run in a straight line, and they raced all the way out of the cave and caught up with Bonnet . . .

. . . while Lavender and Prince Ludwig slowly strolled out of the cave.

'How peaceful it is, out here in the countryside,' said Prince Ludwig.

'Isn't it just?' Lavender replied.

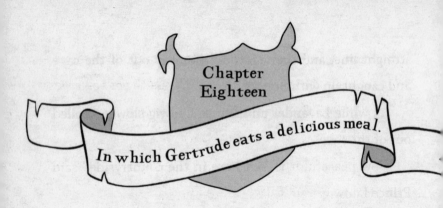

Chapter Eighteen

In which Gertrude eats a delicious meal.

Eliza, Bonnet and Gertrude looked out into the gigantic forest before them. Eliza gulped. They had only gone five metres and already they were a sorry-looking bunch. Eliza's heart was hammering. Bonnet was trembling from bonnet to toe. Gertrude looked as if she'd been haunted by a ghostly acorn.

Of course, Lavender and the prince weren't worried at all. They were having a lovely time. But Eliza knew better. She knew that what lay ahead of them was very, very frightening.

Enormous flowers towered before them. Enormous trees towered before them. An enormous tower towered before them, with an enormous sign on it that read:

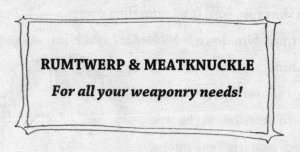

RUMTWERP & MEATKNUCKLE

For all your weaponry needs!

But they were not going to be daunted.

'We are going home,' Eliza said, marching out into the forest.

'Yes we are,' said Bonnet.

'And we're not going to let anything get in our way.'

'No we're not,' said Bonnet.

'We are fearless,' said Eliza.

'We are – Arghhh – dragon!!' Bonnet yelped.

'Oh, honestly, Bonnet,' said Lavender. 'It's not a dragon. It's just quite a big tortoise. Come on!'

'Charming creature,' said Prince Ludwig as they

wandered past the colossal tortoise. Luckily for Bonnet, tortoises, even giant ones, are very slow-moving. And this one seemed completely uninterested in anything other than the crossword it was puzzling over.

'I think four down is *bobble hat*,' said Eliza, as she edged past him.

'I can do this,' Bonnet said to himself as he too inched past the enormous, wrinkly creature. Yes, the trees and plants were enormous. Yes, he could now see a woodlouse that would probably haunt his nightmares forever. And up  in a tree ahead of him, there was a crow staring down at them that didn't even bear thinking about. But he just had to put one foot in front of the other.

'Come on, Bonnet,' he muttered to himself. 'We're in the Land of the Giants. You are a giant. You might be a tiny giant. But you're still a giant. You can lead the way!'

Soon he was striding ahead of everyone else.

'You see!' he said to himself. 'You, Bonnet, are a leader! A hero! You, Bonnet, are a true giant . . .'

'Um, Bonnet?' Eliza said, as calmly as she could. 'You know that hill you're climbing up? With all the mossy black grass on it . . . that's making that loud, rumbling sound?'

'What about it?' said Bonnet breezily. He had reached the peak of the hill and, although he was panting and sweating, he was feeling quite proud of himself.

'Well, don't panic, but it's not actually a hill. It's a giant's belly.'

'Argh!' Bonnet yelled. Luckily for him, that particular giant was fast asleep, and only grunted a little in his sleep as Bonnet skidded and rolled all the way back down his belly to the ground.

It was several hours, a few wrong turnings, four terrifying badgers, and many yelps, shrieks and shudders later that they fought their way through a wall of leaves, and then, with no warning at all, found in front of them . . .

'The cliff! The beanstalk! We've done it!' Eliza gasped.

'We've actually done it,' said Bonnet, hardly able to believe it. There, in front of them, was the edge of the cliff. And there was the top of the beanstalk. As he gazed at it, Bonnet whistled a tune, and ate three scones to celebrate.

'We're going back to Squerb,' Bonnet said. 'That's good, isn't it, Gertrude?'

Gertrude shrugged. She was not a goat who showed strong emotions. But Bonnet was fairly sure that she too was relieved. All they had to do now was climb a few miles down the beanstalk, and they would all be as safe as trousers. He'd never, ever, *ever* have to come back here again.

'I'm sorry for shouting at you before, Lavender,' Eliza said. 'I was just . . . Lavender?'

As she looked around, Eliza felt a cold, icy feeling inside her, as if she'd accidentally eaten a snowman.

Because Lavender and the prince were nowhere to be seen.

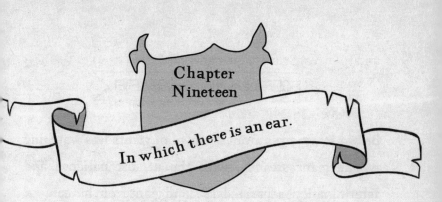

Chapter Nineteen

In which there is an ear.

Lavender and Prince Ludwig were enjoying a lovely evening stroll, oblivious to everything except each other.

'How peaceful it is here,' said Lavender.

'Isn't it just?' Prince Ludwig replied.

They had wandered away from the others some time ago, and had stumbled into a clearing in the forest, with huge banners across it that proclaimed:

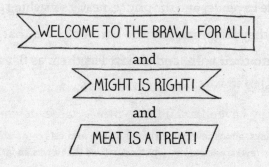

WELCOME TO THE BRAWL FOR ALL!

and

MIGHT IS RIGHT!

and

MEAT IS A TREAT!

and

GET YOUR FREE PUNCH HERE!

Only a few metres away, a crowd of giants was watching as one giant steadily, with the utmost patience and determination, separated a second giant from his ear.

But were Lavender and the prince frightened? Did they hear the *oohs!* and *aahs!*, the roars and grunts? Did they notice the colossal giant's ear soaring through the air and landing on the ground only a few metres away from them? Were they bothered by the river of spilt ale, which sloshed past them, and nearly swept them off their feet?

Did they pay any attention to the two fighting giants, who toppled over as they fought and crashed to the ground just beside Lavender and the prince, nearly squashing them?

Were they frightened by the barrel of wine that came rolling into their path, and almost left them as flat as the earth itself?*

* In those days, almost everyone thought the world was completely flat. Apart from a few rare scientists, who understood that it was, in fact, fizzy.

Of course not.

They only had eyes for each other.

'You know,' said Prince Ludwig. 'I feel like I already know you. Let me guess – you like happiness.'

'I *love* happiness!' Lavender replied.

'And you like wearing pointy hats,' said Prince Ludwig.

'I do!' said Lavender. 'Just like this one I'm wearing now!'

'I knew it!' said Prince Ludwig. 'It's as if we've known each other all our lives. But I want to know more. Tell me all about yourself.'

'Well—' Lavender began.

'You see,' the prince went on, 'I was the first born son of King Alfred and Queen Mabel von Flonderfling. I have seven brothers – Ludwig, Ludwig, Ludwig, Ludwig, Ludwig, Ludwig and—'

'Ludwig?' said Lavender.

The prince beamed at her. 'Yes!' He shook his head at her. 'How could you *possibly* know that? We really must be soulmates. But go on. You were just going to tell me all about yourself.'

'Well, I grew up in a far corner of Squerb, with just one sister,' said Lavender.

'You know, I've often thought about how wonderful it would be to be a peasant, like you,' Prince Ludwig said. 'Just tilling the fields all day. With barely a thought in my tiny little head. Maybe I'd sleep in the stables, just like you . . .'

'Oh, I don't sleep in a stable—'

'And wear rags like yours . . .'

'This is my favourite dress!'

'One day, I could be happy to smell of horse manure, just like you . . .'

'I really don't think I smell like that,' said Lavender.

'But it doesn't matter. Because you're perfect in every way.'

'I am?'

'You really are. I feel so lucky to have found you. Even your name makes me happy. It makes me feel so peaceful.

Colander, Colander, Colander,' said the prince. 'I could say it all day.'

'Um, it's Lavender, not Colander,' said Lavender.

'Of course it is!' said the prince. He sighed. 'You make me so happy.'

'And you make *me* so happy,' Lavender replied. And privately she thanked the Holy Snail, who was still safely stowed in her pocket.

So they strolled along, giddy with happiness.

Only a few metres away, the giants were also rejoicing. For they had just seen one giant bite off another giant's nose.

At the same time, Eliza and Bonnet, who had left Gertrude happily nibbling the beanstalk, were walking back through the woods, shouting.

'Lavender!'

'Prince Ludwig?'

'Lavender?'

'Prince Ludwig!'

'LAVENDER?!'

They shouted until their voices were hoarse. Then some more, until their voices were donkey.

'It's no good,' said Eliza. 'They've vanished.'

'Wait!' said Bonnet. 'I can hear something!'

For now there were twigs crunching, leaves rustling and branches snapping. Eliza and Bonnet looked up hopefully, as two figures sprang out of the undergrowth. Had Lavender and the prince come back?

Er, no.

'Well, well, well. What do we have here, eh, Rumtwerp?' said the first giant.

'Snacks, Meatknuckle. Snacks is what we have here!' said the second giant. 'And to think we were about to go all the way down to the shop. These two will do nicely.'

'Oi!' Meatknuckle pointed at Eliza. 'What flavour are you?'

'Er . . . Old shoes and rats' tails.' Eliza gulped.

'And what about him?' said Meatknuckle, licking his lips as he pointed at Bonnet.

'He tastes more of . . . er, dusty armchairs and . . . unhappy fish,' said Eliza.

'What are the chances, eh, Rumtwerp?' said Meatknuckle. 'Our favourite flavours!'

'Um, Bonnet,' Eliza said, out of the corner of her mouth.
'Bonnet?'

'Mmmmn?'

'RUN!!'

So they ran. Eliza ran as fast as her legs would carry her, and Bonnet raced as fast as his short legs, not very good lungs, and belly full of seventeen scones would carry him.

Rumtwerp and Meatknuckle came after them, shouting, 'Oi! Stop – snacks!'

As they leaped over a busy highway of giant beetles, Eliza had an idea.

'Quick, Bonnet. Get on!'

Eliza jumped on to a passing beetle, pulling Bonnet up after her.

'Where to?' said the beetle.

'Anywhere those giants aren't!' Eliza said.

'Right you are,' the beetle replied. 'Hold on tight.'

Bonnet shut his eyes as the beetle took off, soared up into the air, turned a few circles, and started to fly back towards the two giants.

'Er, could we, um, go *away* from the giants? If that's all right? Not back towards them?' said Bonnet.

'What's that?'

'Away from the giants!' Eliza shouted. 'We need to get *away* from the giants!'

'Don't worry,' said the beetle. 'It's a shortcut.'

'Is it?' said Eliza. 'Because it looks like a shortcut to being eaten!'

But the beetle ignored her, and continued to fly straight at the giants.

They grinned as they saw it coming.

'Are you thinking what I'm thinking?' said Meatknuckle.

'I'm not thinking what you're thinking,' said Rumtwerp, 'because I never think. Waste of time. But what I will shortly be doing is eating. Eating these lovely . . .'

'Snacks!' they said together, as the beetle flew above their heads. They both lunged for it at the same time . . .

KABBLOSH!

. . . missed, and their heads crashed together. As the

beetle rose into the sky, the two giants fell, unconscious, to the ground.

'Er, thanks very much,' Eliza said to the beetle, when they'd landed safely back next to the beanstalk.

'Oh, no trouble,' said the beetle. 'Best of luck now.'

Eliza turned to Gertrude, who had been standing on top of the beanstalk, patiently waiting all this time.

Or, to be more accurate, who had been patiently *eating* all this time. Eating her way through the tasty, chewy plant she was standing on top of.

As Gertrude munched her way through another delicious mouthful of beanstalk, she made quite an amazing noise. First came a low, thunderous rumble, then a loud exploding *boom*, and then there was a slightly mouldly whiff in the air. The beanstalk was clearly having quite a powerful effect on Gertrude's digestion.

'Good mouse – I mean, goat,' said Eliza. She noticed that Gertrude looked less miserable than usual. That was probably something to do with the leaves hanging out of her mouth. And the quantity of beanstalk that she'd already eaten.

Oh no, thought Eliza. *Oh no, no, no, no.*

'Gertrude. Please stop doing that. Right now,' she said, as calmly as she could. For she could see that the beanstalk was now only connected to the top of the cliff by a single stem.

'Gertrude, stop chewing,' she said, more urgently this time. But it would take much more than a few warnings from Eliza to stop Gertrude in the middle of such an excellent meal. The beanstalk, it turned out, tasted like a mixture of apples and old socks – Gertrude's two favourite foods.

So, completely ignoring Eliza, Gertrude chomped her way through the very last stem. The beanstalk was now standing free.

For a moment it stood quite still, perfectly vertical,

all on its own. Then Gertrude's stomach rumbled again. A louder rumble this time, more like an approaching thunderstorm. Another explosion was coming.

Boom. Boom. Ba-boom!

The beanstalk started to lean away from the cliff, slowly at first, and then more quickly. Gertrude found herself moving rapidly sideways . . .

. . . and downwards . . .

. . . which was one very quick way to get back to Squerb, although probably not the one to go for if you still wanted to be breathing at the end of the journey.

'Garghhhk!' cried Gertrude, as she leaped from the collapsing beanstalk. She hurled herself towards the cliff, missed it by an inch . . .

. . . and was only saved by Eliza's hands, clamped tightly around her hoofs.

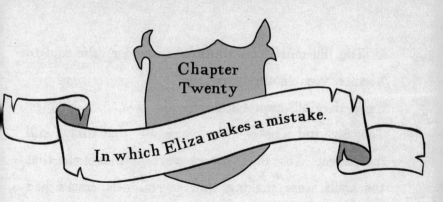

Chapter Twenty

In which Eliza makes a mistake.

There was no way home. Lavender was lost. The forest was dark, and all Eliza could hear were low, ominous mutters coming from Bonnet, and low, ominous rumbles coming from Gertrude's belly, which only reminded her once again that there was no beanstalk, and no way for them ever to get home. Then, suddenly, just as she was climbing over a dozing centipede, Eliza stopped.

She could hear a hideous sound. It sounded like the screams of a thousand angry Vorpels.

'Lavender?' said Eliza. 'It's Lavender! She's singing!'

As Eliza followed the sound, she found, to her surprise, that it was coming from inside a cave. In fact, it was coming from inside the very cave they had escaped from.

'Too Big must have captured Lavender!' she said to Bonnet. 'We've got to rescue her!'

So they all crept back into the cave, past Nibbles, Too Big and Chewy, who were all, thankfully, still fast asleep. Too Big's snores were now so loud that the walls were shaking, and several new cracks had appeared.

'You're alive!' Eliza said, rushing up to her sister. 'I thought you'd been eaten!'

But Lavender ignored her. She was standing outside Old Tumbledown Farm, and gazing at Prince Ludwig, in the middle of a romantic duet.

> 'If a giant puts us in a stew
> You'll still have me, I'll still have you.
> If a giant roasts us on a fire
> That fire won't make our love expire!
> If a giant throws us down a hole
> I'll still love you with all my soul.
> If a giant cooks us in a pie,

Our love will blossom – in that pie.

If we end up on a giant's plate

Well I guess that's just our fate!

Because you're the one for me

And I'm the one for you,

Even if we're in a stew

With mushrooms, thyme and bacon too.

You're the one for me!

And I'm the one for you!

Even if we're in a stew

With mushrooms, thyme and bacon too!'

'Lavender!' hissed Eliza. 'What happened? How were you captured?'

'Captured?' said Lavender. 'I wasn't captured! We just went for a walk . . . and then came back.'

'Wait . . . what?' said Eliza. 'You mean you came back here *on purpose*?'

'Well, this is our house, isn't it?' said Lavender.

Eliza gaped at her sister, speechless for a moment.

'It didn't occur to you that if you came back into the cave you might get eaten. Or squashed. Or crushed?'

'Well, no,' said Prince Ludwig politely, with a broad, Ludwiggy* smile on his face.

'No,' said Eliza. 'Of course not! Why would it? I mean, there are only two giants and one monumental beast in here!'

'Exactly!' said Prince Ludwig, gazing at her with all the intelligence of a meringue. Then he frowned, as he noticed that Eliza was staring at him with the same intense stare that his great-aunt Bertha sometimes gave him when he'd used the wrong fork at dinner.

'Saliva,' Prince Ludwig began, 'there's no need to worry.'

'It's Eliza, not Saliva,' said Eliza.

'Of course. Saliva and Sonnet,' said Prince Ludwig.

'*Eliza* and *Bonnet*,' growled Eliza.

'Indeed. There is no need to worry. For I will stay awake all night,' he said. 'I myself will guard your extremely humble shack. It will be a test of my love for Violet.'

* A word for incredibly empty-headed – that Eliza just made up.

'Er, it's Lavender,' said Lavender.

'Of course. Lavender! Now go inside, all of you, while I stand guard. That is my solemn vow.'

'Thank you, my prince,' said Lavender.

So she followed the others inside, while Prince Ludwig stood by the front door to guard them. He wondered how he would spend the long, lonely hours ahead. Perhaps he would compose a love poem. *Labrador, Labrador*, he began . . .

'You see?' said Lavender as she sat down on her bed. 'Everything's worked out perfectly.' Then she wondered why her sister was staring at her like an angry gorilla.

'What is wrong with you?!' Eliza exploded. 'You came back here *on purpose*! Did your brain melt like a cheese in the sun?'

Lavender just smiled back at her.

Eliza clenched her fists. Why was her sister like this? Didn't she understand that they were trying to get home? Or was she so in love with the prince that her brain had just stopped working?

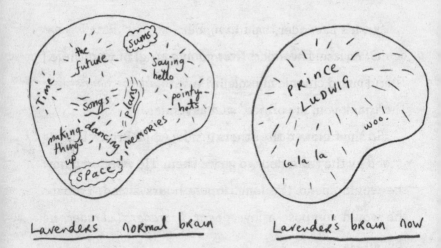

Lavender's normal brain

Lavender's brain now

'Eliza, why do you always worry so much? Everything's going to be fine.'

'No it's not! It's not going to be fine! We're all going to be EATEN!'

'But don't you see,' said Lavender. 'This is just like a fairy tale! It's magical!'

'Enough!' said Eliza. 'Please. Just. Leave. Me. Alone.'

'But—'

'Don't say another word.'

'Not even "fairy tale"?'

'Especially not "fairy tale".'

As Lavender left the room, Eliza sighed. Finally she could work out how they were going to get out of here. There had to be a way home. Even without the beanstalk. There just *had* to be. But what was it?

Eliza put on her thinking cap.

When that didn't have any effect, she tried out her strategy hat. Nope. Finally she put on her disaster helmet.

← thinking cap

strategy hat ↓

← disaster helmet

Still nothing.

So she tried to imagine what Grandma Maud would say to her, if she was here. 'Oh, don't worry about it, dear, you'll probably get eaten soon enough. Just enjoy the time you have left.'

Yes, that was exactly what Grandma Maud would say.

Which was no use whatsoever.

So she tiptoed out of the house and started to draw a list of escape plans on the cave wall. As Chewy, Too Big and Nibbles all grunted and snored in their sleep, Eliza scribbled and paced, and scribbled and paced.

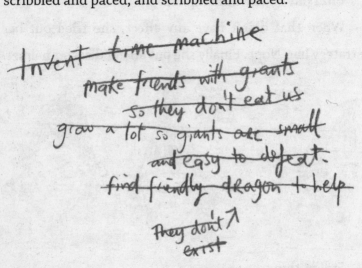

~~Invent time machine~~

make friends with giants
~~so they don't eat us~~
grow a lot so giants ~~are small~~
~~and easy to defeat.~~

~~find friendly dragon + help~~

They don't ↗
exist

Finally, she had a plan.

1. Panic
2. Get Eaten

'Eliza?'

Eliza whirled around, to see her sister standing there, looking particularly sheepish.

'I have something to tell you,' Lavender said.

'Unless it's an amazing escape plan, I don't want to hear it,' said Eliza.

'Actually,' said Lavender. 'I *can* get us all home. You see . . . It's my fault that we're here at all.'

'What?'

This was not going to be easy, Lavender knew that.

'Why don't I explain everything with a song?' she said nervously.

'Please don't!' said Eliza. But Lavender had already begun.

> *One day I found a little snail*
> *(This is quite an unusual tale)*
> *The creature was a **magic** snail*
> *(It even had a magic trail)*
> *And with this snail I cast a spell*

Because I thought: "All will be well
If I can find myself a prince"—'

'Lavender!' Eliza said. 'Shhhh! You'll wake up Too Big! And Nibbles! Just tell me in plain, simple words! No singing, *please*!'

So Lavender took a small wooden box out of her pocket, opened it up, and told Eliza everything. She told her about Sybil, and about the three magical wishes, and how her first wish had come true.

'So you see, I still have two wishes left,' Lavender said. 'I can take us all home! I was just distracted before, because of Prince Ludwig, with his perfect face, and his perfect ears, and his perfect chin, and his perfect eyebrows, and his perfect elbows, and—'

'Enough!'

'Anyway. He seemed quite perfect. Only he kept calling me Labrador. But I still thought he was my true love. Until he offered to keep us all safe by standing guard.'

'And?'

'Well . . .'

Eliza followed Lavender's gaze as she looked over to Old Tumbledown Farm. Outside it she could see Prince Ludwig fast asleep, face down on the ground. Nearby, trembling from head to foot, there was *someone* standing guard. It just happened to be Bonnet.

'So I thought,' said Lavender. 'Perhaps Prince Ludwig isn't my true love after all. And perhaps snails aren't always a girl's best friend, and – why are you looking at me like that?'

'Sorry, Lavender, but you really expect me to believe that a snail's magic brought us here?' said Eliza, plucking the snail out of the small wooden box.

'Yes!' said Lavender. 'It's the Holy Snail.'

'Oh *really*,' said Eliza.

'Yes!' said Lavender.

'The Holy Snail,' said Eliza.

'That is correct,' said Sybil. 'I am the Holy Snail. Please be careful with me. I may be magical, but my shell is still quite fragile.'

Eliza blinked. She looked down at the snail. The snail looked back up at her.

'It's all perfectly true,' Sybil went on. 'Lavender said the magic words, "I wish." Then I simply made it all come true.'

'But. But – but . . .'

Now Eliza's mind was boggling. Her brain was bending. Her world was wiggling.

'So you're saying, Lavender, that you *planned* all this?'

'Well, sort of,' said Lavender.

'And you didn't tell me?'

'Yeah . . .' said Lavender.

'But – we could have been eaten alive!'

'Mmmnn . . .'

'Or squashed!'

'Yeah . . .'

'Or just accidentally sat on.'

'True . . .'

'Seriously. Did your brain shrink to the size of a pea? Did you not think at all? Or have you swapped brains with a pigeon?'

'Um . . . I don't think so,' said Lavender.

'Although if you were a pigeon,' said Eliza, 'you wouldn't be able to do crazy things like this. You know what? I wish you *were* a pigeon. That would make my life a whole lot easier!!'

Eliza breathed out. She felt a little bit better.

'Well?' she said. 'Don't you have anything to say for yourself? Lavender?'

She looked around. How did her sister always manage to disappear at precisely the wrong moment?

'So that's it,' Eliza said. 'Very grown-up of you. You're not going to apologize. You're just going to hide.'

'Not much point talking to her now,' said a small, calm voice.

'What?' said Eliza, looking down at the snail in her hands.

'Not much point talking to her now,' said Sybil, cheerfully. 'Oh, by the way, your wish has been granted. One more to go.'

'Wish? What wish? What do you mean, "One more to go"?'

The snail shrugged, and smiled. 'Look up,' she said, before shrinking back into her shell.

'What are you talking about?' said Eliza. She looked up.

'Oh no. Oh no. No. NO!'

For sitting on top of Old Tumbledown Farm was something that definitely hadn't been there before. An enormous grey pigeon.

'Lavender?'

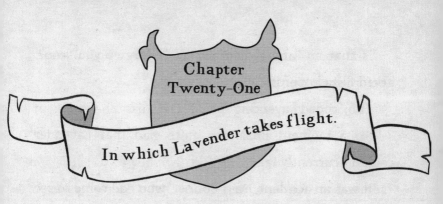

Chapter
Twenty-One

In which Lavender takes flight.

Sometimes it's hard to find the right words to say sorry. Perhaps if greetings cards existed in the Land of the Giants, that might have helped. But to be honest, Eliza was never really going to find one that said 'SO SORRY . . . FOR TURNING YOU INTO A MASSIVE PIGEON'.

Eliza had to say *something* though.

'I'm *really* sorry,' said Eliza, staring up at the large, grey bird that was perched on top of Old Tumbledown Farm. 'All you wanted was to be a tiny creature, like Thumbelina. Instead you ended up as . . . Well, as . . . this.'

'Coo,' cooed Lavender.

'I really didn't mean to do that.'

'Coo.'

'Is that an "angry" coo? Or an "I forgive you" coo?' asked Eliza hopefully.

'Coo,' cooed Lavender.

For a moment Eliza was quite glad that Lavender couldn't currently talk.

'It was an accident,' said Bonnet, who had come to see what all the shouting was about. 'Really, Lavender, it, er . . . suits you,' he said. 'And on the bright side, now you can fly! And, um, speak pigeon, which might be fun if you ever, um . . . meet other pigeons,' he said uncertainly.

'Coo,' Lavender replied.

Bonnet didn't know exactly what Lavender was saying. But he had a feeling that she wasn't very impressed.

'Coo,' cooed Lavender again.

Eliza's face lit up. 'But of course! Everything's going to be fine! I've still got the Holy Sna—aaarghh!'

Eliza yelped as Nibbles appeared out of nowhere and launched herself at Lavender.

As Lavender fluttered out of reach, Nibbles crashed into the house, leaving a large, monster-cat-shaped dent in the wall. Nibbles leaped away, snarling, and then crouched low, her eyes fixed on the tasty-looking pigeon now hopping from one foot to the other in front of the house and looking distinctly ruffled.

'Get back, Nibbles!' Eliza shouted, putting herself between her sister and the giant, hissing beast.

Behind her, Bonnet was flapping his arms. And, behind him, Lavender was flapping her wings.

Flap. Flap. How do wings work, anyway? Like this? Yes.

Lavender took off, flew up into the air, then landed on her side almost immediately.

Flap, flap, flap, fly – this time she crashed into Old Tumbledown Farm.

'Fly, Lavender, fly!' her sister was shouting.

She tried again, and this time everything seemed to be working better. Except for one small detail. As she flapped her wings and flew up into the air, Lavender realized that there was something attached to her foot. And that something was her sister.

'Urghh – maybe this wasn't the best idea,' Eliza gasped,

as the ground slipped away below her. She had been scared that Lavender would fly out of the cave, and that she'd never see her again. After all, Lavender had developed quite a habit of disappearing recently.

But now Lavender was flying around the cave in a mad panic, with Eliza underneath her swinging about wildly.

'I'm sorry, Lavender!' Eliza yelled as they careered through the air, with all the grace of a blindfolded badger falling down a flight of stairs.

Nibbles was still staring up at the pigeon, with a look of determined hatred and hunger on her face.

But Nibbles was no longer the problem.

Flying was the problem. Eliza shut her eyes as Lavender flew straight up in the air, then dived down and started a series of acrobatic loops that most ordinary pigeons would have been quite proud of.

Is this up? thought

Lavender. *No – this is up! This is it! I'm getting the hang of it! Ha! I'm getting it! Yes! I can fly!* she thought, just as she crashed, beak first, into Too Big's wall of weapons.

There was a loud clatter as Lavender, Eliza, a club and eleven spears went crashing to the ground. As Eliza lay dazed on the floor, she noticed that the room seemed to be spinning.

'Why are there so many stars inside?' she murmured, just before her eyes shut.

As she lay on the floor, dreaming of gentle giants who just wanted to give humans piggybacks, the Holy Snail slid out of her hand and went gliding away across the floor.

Sybil was searching for something. Was it a mysterious magical object? Was Sybil herself setting out on a magical quest?

No. Not really. She was just quite hungry.

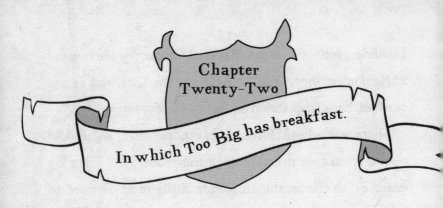

Chapter Twenty-Two

In which Too Big has breakfast.

In the morning, Too Big was in a cheerful mood. Some people, and even some giants, get nervous before competitions. But not Too Big. He knew he was going to win the Brawl For All. He just had to practise a bit of terrifying bellowing and a little light axe flinging, and he would be all set. Best of all, he had received a good omen. A great big, juicy pigeon had flown into his cave in the middle of the night.

He had popped the plump little creature into a cage, and now it was hanging from the ceiling, just waiting to be grilled. Yes, it was going to be a wonderful morning, and he couldn't wait to get out there and start thumping and crunching and whacking!

Eliza, on the other hand, was not having such a happy morning.

First she'd woken up on the floor of the cave to find that the Holy Snail was missing.

Then Eliza, Bonnet and Gertrude had started to search for the Holy Snail. Eliza had tried to get the prince to help them, but he wouldn't wake up.*

Meanwhile, from inside her cage, hanging far above them, Lavender let out a series of melancholy 'coos'.

'Don't worry!' Eliza whispered up to her. 'We're going to find the snail, and then we'll get you out of there!'

Luckily Too Big and Chewy were still snoring away like angry hippos, and Nibbles was lying on the floor, purring loudly as she snoozed.

So they looked and looked, but in the darkness they couldn't find the snail anywhere. There was *one* place they

---

* Waking up was not something Prince Ludwig had ever achieved without the help of his butler, twelve trumpeters and a slice of hot apple pie.

hadn't looked – on top of Too Big's breakfast table. So Gertrude shimmied up on to the tabletop, faster than you could say whirling dandytrousers, with Bonnet and Eliza on her back.

'As long as they don't wake up,' Bonnet muttered as they crept over the table, 'everything's going to be – uh-oh.'

For that was the moment the snoring stopped. Then Too Big stretched, yawned, shook his head and plodded over to the breakfast table.

'Breakfast time, Chewy!' he shouted, tossing some logs on to the fire. 'Wakey-wakey! It's my big day!'

On the tabletop Eliza, Bonnet and Gertrude stood completely still as Chewy ran over to the breakfast table, grinning.

If he sees us, Eliza thought, *then that's it. We'll be done for. We'll be . . . breakfast.* She looked around for a place to hide. There was a bowl of salt on the table. As Too Big threw some chicken drumsticks on to the fire, Eliza, Bonnet and Gertrude climbed into the bowl, took a deep breath and then dived into the salt.

'What do you want for breakfast, Chew-chew?' said Too Big. 'Chicken beaks? Oxen ears? Shark steaks? Freshly grilled pigeon?'

Inside the salt bowl Eliza's heart skipped a beat. *Freshly grilled pigeon?*

'Pigeons are yucky,' said Chewy. 'Chicken beaks, please!'

'Suit yourself,' Too Big replied. 'I'll have the pigeon later. It'll make a tasty victory snack.'

Eliza wanted to breathe a sigh of relief. Unfortunately she couldn't breathe any kind of sigh at all. She couldn't hold her breath for much longer. *Please leave*, she thought – as Too Big dug his spoon into the salt and lifted Bonnet out.

Bonnet froze with fear. He clung to the spoon and tried his very best to look like salt. Luckily for Bonnet, Too Big was still a bit sleepy. He wasn't paying that much attention as he sprinkled salt all over his drumsticks, and he didn't notice a thing as Bonnet jumped off the spoon and ran to hide behind a nearby flagon.

Then he lay down on the tabletop, doing his best impression of a fork.

'Right,' said Too Big. 'Time to prove what I always say . . .'

'If at first you don't succeed, hit everybody harder?' said Chewy.

'And?'

'Might is right?' said Chewy.

'And?'

'If you can't beat 'em, bash 'em?' said Chewy.

'And?'

Well, that's it, Eliza thought. She couldn't hold her breath any longer. If she opened her mouth, she'd get a mouthful of salt. Nearby she could hear Gertrude making small spluttering sounds.

Is it better to suffocate in a bowl of salt or get eaten by a giant? Neither of them sound that much fun. Oh well. Goodbye, world. Goodbye, Gertrude. Goodbye, Bonnet. Goodbye, Lavender, sister, friend and pigeon . . .

'Sticks and stones may break my bones, but clubs and

spears are spikier!' Chewy said joyfully.

'That's my girl,' roared Too Big. 'Come on! Let's show the world who's boss!'

Then Too Big stood up, plucked his favourite club off the wall, whirled it in the air and set off out of the cave. Chewy ran along beside him, whirling her (much smaller) club in the air.

Inside the cave, Eliza and Gertrude gasped as they burst out of the salt. Gertrude shook herself and sneezed, spraying salt everywhere.

'We're alive!' Eliza grinned. 'And they've gone! And – that is a great fork impression, Bonnet!'

Eliza wanted to celebrate. But there was no time to waste. She had to get her sister out of the cage. She climbed out of the salt bowl and shimmied down from the breakfast table on Gertrude's back.

'Now all I have to do is slice through that rope,' she explained to Bonnet. 'Then the cage will fall to the floor.'

'I'm sure it will all be fine,' said Bonnet. 'Unless you shoot your sister in the head.'

'Thanks, Bonnet,' said Eliza.

'Or in the foot. Or any other part of her. Just try to not shoot her. But I'm sure you won't,' he added, sounding not very sure at all.

'*Thanks*, Bonnet,' said Eliza. She shut one eye and focused on the rope. *Do not miss. Do not miss.* But just as she was about to release the arrow, Bonnet cried out.

'Nibbles!' he yelled as the hideous beast sprang towards them. Eliza turned to look and, as she did, she accidentally released the arrow.

Peong!

Bonnet and Eliza watched
helplessly as the arrow soared
through the air. Time seemed
to slow down as it sped closer
and closer to Lavender . . .
missed the cage by an inch
and sliced the rope above the
cage in two.

The cage tumbled through

the air, landing squarely on Nibbles's head.

CLANG!

The beast let out a hideous squeal and shot from the cave. And as the cage crashed on to the ground it broke open and Lavender came hopping out of it, cooing appreciatively.

'Lavender!' cried Eliza.

'Coo!' Lavender replied.

'Now all we have to do is get that snail,' said Eliza. 'It's got to be here somewhere. Then we can turn Lavender back to – well, to Lavender. And get home!'

So they searched under Chewy's bed. They searched through the glowing embers of Too Big's fire. They even looked under Nibbles's tail (luckily, the beast was fast asleep). They trawled through Too Big's gigantic pile of dirty tunics, and through Chewy's box of broken toys.

But the snail was nowhere to be seen.

'That's it,' said Eliza miserably. 'It's gone. We're never going to get home. And Lavender will never quite be Lavender again.'

'Coo,' cooed Lavender.

Bonnet sat down next to Eliza.

'This can't have happened,' he said. 'It *hasn't* happened.'

'But it *has* happened. And there's nothing to be done,' said Eliza. 'Everything's ruined. And it's all my fault. We're all going to get eaten.'

'We might not get eaten,' said Bonnet, trying to be hopeful. 'We might get squashed first.'

'Good point,' said Eliza.

'Grgghk,' grunted Gertrude, in agreement.

Eliza stared down at the ground as a shaft of sunlight lit up the cave. *Odd,* Eliza thought. *My mind must be playing tricks on me*. Last night she was seeing stars in the roof of the cave. And now in the warm morning light she was seeing stars on the floor.

Was it her imagination, or was the floor sparkling?

'Bonnet,' she said quietly. 'Look down.'

'What?' said Bonnet. When he looked down, all he saw was his small, hairy feet. Like many things in life, they frightened him.

'No, Bonnet – at the floor!' said Eliza. 'Look! Do you see that sparkly path, zigzagging across the floor?'

'Mmmhmmm,' said Bonnet.

Suddenly Eliza was on her feet. 'Don't you see?' she said. 'The silvery path – it's a snail trail! The Holy Snail's trail! We just have to find out where it ends! If we find the Holy Snail, we can make the third wish, and then we can get home!'

So they followed the sparkly trail across the floor. And back again. And up Too Big's wall of weapons, where the trail looped, and zigzagged, and . . . stopped.

'That's the space where Too Big's club should be,' said Eliza, with a shudder. 'Which means . . .'

'That the Holy Snail is on Too Big's club,' said Bonnet.

'Then we've got to get to that snail before he smashes it to pieces!'

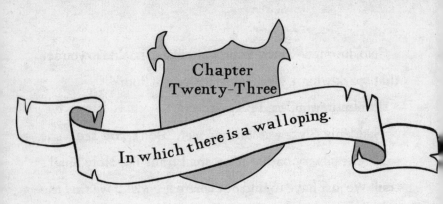

Chapter Twenty-Three

In which there is a walloping.

'Too – Big! Too – Big! TOO – BIG!' the crowd cheered.

In the clearing, not far from the cave, a disaster* of giants had gathered. There were hairy giants, scary giants, craggy giants and saggy giants. The polite, gentle giants could not be seen. Mainly because they didn't exist.

As the Championship began, Too Big made short work of the first couple of rounds. He smashed his way through the Chair Breaking round. He nailed the Squid Hurling round.

* A giant word for 'more than a hundred giants'.

160

He wiped the floor with his rivals in the Extreme Mopping round.

He won the Speed Chess round in record time, by simply eating the chess set.

Next up was the semi final: the Staring Contest. That was easy – he just gave all his rivals black eyes, so none of them could see.

Now there was just one round left. There were only two other competitors in the final – a pair of complete boneheads called Rumtwerp and Meatknuckle. Too Big wasn't worried. He was the most frightening giant in all the land. Rumtwerp and Meatknuckle would be so scared of him they wouldn't stand a chance.

'Time for the Great Wallop!' the judge announced. 'Let's have a round of applause for Rumtwerp, Meatknuckle and our defending champion – Too Big!'

Too Big grinned, and roared, and flexed his muscles, as the crowd yelled out his name. *This is going to be easy-peasy*, Too Big thought. He didn't notice – and why would he? – a small grey bird, flying towards him. If he had noticed it, he might have been distracted by all sorts of questions. Like: *Where have I seen that bird before?* And: *Does that bird really have two tiny humans and a mouse riding on its back?*

'Too – Big! Too – Big! Too – Big!' the crowd cheered.

'Down there!' shouted Eliza, holding on tight, as Lavender soared through the air. 'I can see it! He's got it! He's got the Holy Snail!'

And sure enough, the Holy Snail was sitting on a tasty green leaf, on the end of a small brown branch, attached to Too Big's club.*

'Can you see it, Bonnet?' Eliza shouted, as they soared through the air. 'Can you see the Holy Snail?'

'Er . . . Yeah!' Bonnet lied. Sitting behind Eliza, with the wind blowing in his face, he had his eyes shut tight. He knew that very soon he was going to have to be brave. Braver than he'd ever been in his life. So he decided not

---

* Sybil was feeling quite pleased with herself. After Lavender had forgotten to feed her, she had searched high and low before she found the only green leaf in the whole of Too Big's cave. Now she was enjoying her breakfast.

to open his eyes quite yet. He didn't want to use up all his bravery in one go.

Down below them, a voice thundered: 'This is it! The Great Wallop! The Grand Finale of the Brawl For All! The walloping rules are these. If you die, you lose. If you cry, you lose. The wallop will end when just one giant is left standing. Or when I get bored and want to go home. Clubs at the ready! On your marks, get, set . . .'

'Aarrgh!' cried Too Big. For just as he raised his club, ready for the biggest walloping of his life, a most unexpected event took place.

Something landed on his head.

'Aaargh!' he yelped, trying to shake it off. 'What is that?'

'Oh, it's only a pigeon,' said Bonnet, as he jumped down from the pigeon on to Too Big's left shoulder.

'You!' raged Too Big. 'What are *you* doing here?!'

Meanwhile, Rumtwerp and Meatknuckle hadn't even noticed that Too Big was apparently talking to himself. They were too busy whacking each other as hard as they could.

THWACK!

BOSH!

KERPLUNK!

PAZZOW!

But the crowd were no longer paying any attention to them. They were all staring as Too Big jumped up and down and hopped from one foot to the other, as he tried, unsuccessfully, to get the pigeon off his head. When he tried to brush it away, it flew up into the air. A moment later, it landed again.

As he got angrier and angrier with the pigeon, someone in the audience laughed. There was a loud gasp. Nobody ever laughed at Too Big.

'We just wanted to help you win the Brawl For All!' said Eliza, who was sitting on top of Gertrude, on Too Big's right shoulder. 'We thought it was only fair. Since we belong to you.'

'Fair? What is this word, "fair"?!' spluttered Too Big. 'Get it OFF me!'

'Oh, aren't you pleased?' Eliza replied. 'We just brought our lucky, er, mouse – *and* our lucky pigeon to be your mascots.'

'Just get that thing off my head, before I EAT ALL OF YOU!' Too Big roared.

'But if you eat us,' said Bonnet, 'you won't get the good luck. Oh, I almost forgot. The luckiest thing of all is when a pigeon poops on your head!'

'What?' boomed Too Big. 'Don't even think—'

But it was too late. He could already feel a dollop of warm gooey liquid spreading on top of his head. Now it was slowly sliding down his forehead.

'Arghhh!' he roared.

The crowd of giants were all starting to giggle. This was an unusual sensation for them. It was quite different from roaring, grunting or yelling. But they found that it was really quite pleasant. Even Rumtwerp and Meatknuckle had taken a break from beating each other up to join in.

'Aren't you so glad you came and took our house?' said Eliza.

'No I am NOT glad, you stupid little teeny-tinies!' he howled. 'You are the worst presents ever!!'

'Oh,' said Eliza. 'And we were just starting to enjoy ourselves. Are you sure you don't secretly really like us?'

'Arrrghhh!' roared Too Big. 'NO!! I DO NOT SECRETLY LIKE YOU, YOU TEENY-TINY IDIOT! I WISH I'D NEVER EVER PICKED UP YOUR STUPID LITTLE SHACK IN THE FIRST PLACE!'

As he said those words, Eliza and Bonnet looked at each other – and grinned.

There was a flash. Then a bang. All of a sudden, all the teeny-tiny creatures and the small grey pigeon simply vanished.

'Hey!' said Too Big. 'Stop hiding! What did you do? Come back here! How dare you disappear! I'm going to get you and I'm going to – uh oh . . .'

Too Big was about to say 'eat you', but he didn't get the chance. Because just then he noticed Rumtwerp and Meatknuckle raising their clubs, about to give him the walloping of his life.

'Er . . .'

In the end, Too Big had an utterly miserable morning. He did still win a cup. But it wasn't the one he was hoping for.

FASTEST AT RUNNING AWAY

And as she watching her father fleeing the clearing, Chewy began to realize that maybe, just maybe, 'hitting everybody' wasn't the answer to everything, after all.

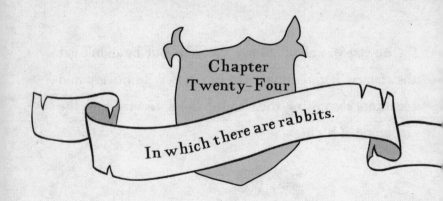

Chapter Twenty-Four

In which there are rabbits.

There was only one person in the whole Land of the Giants who had a more miserable morning than Too Big. And that was Boris. The Holy Snail was nowhere to be found, and she was finding it hard to remain calm. Doris and Horace weren't being much help either.*

As the carpet soared through the air, Boris couldn't help muttering to herself.

'Typical. Typical! You just had to ruin everything, didn't you? You had the most precious object in the whole of Squerb. But you lost it! You went and lost it, because you are an idiot, Boris. You're just a complete, utter, total—'

* In fairness, that wasn't really their fault, since she had turned them both into rabbits.

168

And then, all of a sudden, everything went quiet.

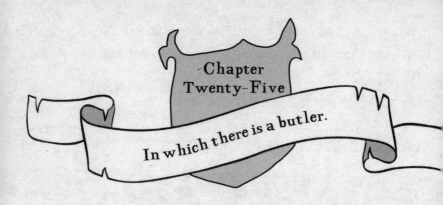

Chapter Twenty-Five

In which there is a butler.

Meanwhile, Prince Ludwig awoke and was delighted to find himself back in his very own kingdom.

'You know, I met the most wonderful girl,' he told his butler, Godfrey. 'She will be forever imprinted on my memory. I must find her again!'

'It shall be done, Your Highness,' Godfrey replied. 'Simply tell me her name, and she will be found.'

'Well, she comes from the realm of Squid, and her name is Raveller. I think. Or – was it Conifer? No! Pamela. Hold on – I think it was Jennifer. No, no – I know. Caliper! No. Bannister! That was it. Bannister. From Squid.'

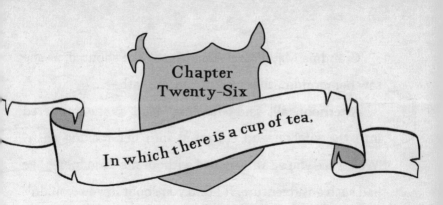

Chapter Twenty-Six

In which there is a cup of tea,

Meanwhile, in a far corner of the kingdom, deep in the realm of Squerb, Old Tumbledown Farm was back where it belonged. The chimney was restored, the front door was back on, the giant cat-shaped dent in the wall was gone. And everyone was safe and sound, as if Too Big had never stolen their house in the first place.

'Home!' Eliza said. 'We did it!'

'We did it!' Lavender and Bonnet agreed.

Eliza had never been so happy to look out of the window, and see the grey cloudy sky, the overgrown garden, and the dark, gloomy forest beyond it. She had never been so happy to smell the muddy, grassy, slightly-manurey smell of their backyard, and—

'Grandma Maud! Grandma Maud!' she shouted, as she saw her grandmother walking up the path.

'Afternoon, all,' said Grandma Maud, as she wandered into the kitchen and collapsed into her rocking chair. 'Well, I see you've all survived without me. Goodness, I've had such an adventure. If I told you about it, you wouldn't believe me, not for a second.'

'Why – what happened?' asked Eliza.

'Well,' said Grandma Maud. 'It was just as I predicted. I saw The End of the World.'

'The End of the World?' said Eliza, frowning.

'Oh yes. It was quite wonderful. You know what I saw? The rabbits of the apocalypse, flying past on their Carpet of Catastrophe.'

'Right,' said Eliza. She and Bonnet exchanged glances.

'And then I drank a little brandy. Just one sip for every year since the world began. And then I felt a little sleepy – that must have been because of the apocalypse.'

'Definitely,' said Eliza.

'And then everything went black. You see?'

'Er, not really,' said Eliza.

'The world ended, my dear. I'd tell you more, but you wouldn't understand. No spirit of adventure, that's the trouble with you,' she said, with a yawn.

'But, Grandma Maud,' said Eliza. 'The world didn't end, did it?'

'It certainly did,' said Grandma Maud.

'But if the world has ended,' Eliza persisted, 'then how are we still here?'

'Oh, that's quite simple. The world ended. And then a new one began, just afterwards. Take a look around. Everything might look the same to you. But not to me. Look at your sister, out there in the garden! She's drinking out of a puddle!'

'Oh yes, so she is,' said Eliza, looking out of the window. Lavender had indeed slipped out into the garden. And she was now bending over a puddle, sipping water from it.

'You see? I told you so. We are in a new world.'

'Er . . .' said Eliza. She could have explained the whole

story to her grandma. But it just seemed much, much simpler not to.

The next morning, Lavender and Bonnet were sitting on the roof. It was Lavender's new favourite place. She liked the feeling of space it gave her.

'Are you all right, Lavender?' said Bonnet.

'I'm completely all right,' said Lavender, 'and totally back to normal. Although it is a bit sad not to be able to fly any more. Oh . . . and I seem to have acquired a taste for worms.'

'What was that?' said Bonnet. 'I thought you just said "worms".'

'Mmmn,' said Lavender. 'They're so juicy. And earthy. I don't know why princesses never eat them. I've got a whole bowlful. Would you like one?'

'Er . . . Not right now,' said Bonnet.

'So, um . . . do you mind that Prince Ludwig has gone back to his own kingdom?' Bonnet asked.

'Not really,' said Lavender, with a smile. 'I don't want

to go to any more faraway kingdoms.'

'No?'

'No. And I don't want to marry a prince anymore.'

'You don't?' said Bonnet, hopefully.

'No, I want to stay right here,' said Lavender. 'In The Back of Beyond, with everyone I care about. Eliza and Grandma Maud, and you, obviously . . .'

'Me?' said Bonnet, blushing like a robin,* and thinking

---

* Not many people know this, but robins are red because they are permanently embarrassed. They're not actually called Robin. They're called Arnold. But they're too polite to say so.

how beautiful Lavender looked as she helped herself to another generous mouthful of worms.

'Of course,' said Lavender. 'I don't know what I'd do without you.'

Bonnet's stomach flipped over like an excitable young pancake. This was his moment. The moment for him to say everything he wanted to say to Lavender. He wasn't sure exactly what that was. But he did know it would include words like 'wondrous' and 'loveliness', and phrases like 'happy as a scone', and 'I might go easy on the worms, if I were you.'

He took a deep breath.

'Lavender,' he began.

'And Gertrude, of course,' said Lavender. 'I don't know what I'd do without Gertrude either.'

Down in the garden, Gertrude gave a little grunt of appreciation as she tucked into another delicious bonnet.

'Of course,' said Bonnet, sighing. 'We mustn't forget Gertrude. Lovely, lovely Gertrude.'

About the Author

Sarah Courtauld lives in London, where she writes sentences with all sorts of words in them – nouns, verbs, adjectives – occasionally even her favourite word, 'parcel'. She owns more pencils than is strictly necessary and can often be found drawing the goats in her local park. Her favourite cheese is 'all of them'.

Goth Girl

and the Wuthering Fright

CHRIS RIDDELL

From the winner of the Costa Children's Book Award

The most esteemed authors
in the world are coming to show
off their pampered pooches at the

Ghastly-Gorm Hall
literary dog show.

But there's something strange afoot at
Ghastly-Gorm – mysterious paw prints, howls in
the night and some suspiciously chewed shoes.
Can Ada work out what's going on
before the next full moon?

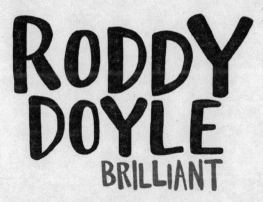

RODDY DOYLE

BRILLIANT

Gloria and Rayzer must save their Uncle Ben. The black dog has got him. That's what they heard their granny say anyway. And, she says, it's taken Dublin's funny bone too.

Gloria and Rayzer are really brave, but the black dog is scary and they can't fight it alone. Soon Dublin's children are helping . . . And then the animals in Dublin Zoo . . . And some cheeky seagulls as well. But could the biggest help of all be an ordinary word shouted – as loudly as possible – by all the kids together?

MY BIG FAT ZOMBIE GOLDFISH

MO O'HARA

THIS FISH JUST GOT NASTY!

When Tom's big brother dunks Frankie the goldfish into toxic green gunge, Tom zaps the fish with a battery to bring him back to life! But there's something weird about the new Frankie – he's now a BIG FAT ZOMBIE GOLDFISH with hypnotic powers . . . and he's out for revenge.

TWO BIG FAT FISHY STORIES THAT WILL KEEP YOU HOOKED AND MAKE YOU LAUGH OUT LOUD!

WWW.GOBSTOPPERBOOKS.COM

VISIT THE GOBSTOPPERS WEBSITE FOR

AUTHOR NEWS · BONUS CONTENT
VIDEOS · GAMES · PRIZES . . .
AND MORE!

MACMILLAN
Children's Books